Other books by J. D. Salinger:

The Catcher in the Rye
Nine Stories
Raise High the Roof Beam, Carpenters *and*
    Seymour: An Introduction

Franny
and
Zooey

J. D. Salinger

BANTAM BOOKS
TORONTO • NEW YORK • LONDON • SYDNEY • AUCKLAND

*This low-priced Bantam Book
has been completely reset in a type face
designed for easy reading, and was printed
from new plates. It contains the complete
text of the original hard-cover edition.*
NOT ONE WORD HAS BEEN OMITTED.

RL 7, IL 10+

FRANNY AND ZOOEY

*A Bantam Book / published by arrangement with
Little, Brown and Company, Inc.*

PRINTING HISTORY
Little, Brown edition published September 1961

2nd printing . September 1961	7th printing . November 1961
3rd printing . September 1961	8th printing . . . January 1962
4th printing . . . October 1961	9th printing . . February 1962
5th printing . . . October 1961	10th printing . . . . March 1962
6th printing . . . October 1961	11th printing . . . August 1962

12th printing . . . October 1962

"Franny" appeared in THE NEW YORKER *January 1955*
"Zooey" appeared in THE NEW YORKER *May 1957*
*Bantam edition / February 1964
40 printings through October 1985*

ISBN 0-553-20348-7

Published simultaneously in the United States and Canada

---

*Bantam Books are published by Bantam Books, Inc. Its trade-
mark, consisting of the words "Bantam Books" and the por-
trayal of a rooster, is Registered in U.S. Patent and Trademark
Office and in other countries. Marca Registrada. Bantam
Books, Inc., 666 Fifth Avenue, New York, New York 10103.*

PRINTED IN THE UNITED STATES OF AMERICA

H   48 47 46 45 44 43 42

As nearly as possible in the spirit of Matthew Salinger, age one, urging a luncheon companion to accept a cool lima bean, I urge my editor, mentor and (heaven help him) closest friend, William Shawn, *genius domus* of *The New Yorker,* lover of the long shot, protector of the unprolific, defender of the hopelessly flamboyant, most unreasonably modest of born great artist-editors, to accept this pretty skimpy-looking book.

Franny

THOUGH brilliantly sunny, Saturday morning was overcoat weather again, not just topcoat weather, as it had been all week and as everyone had hoped it would stay for the big weekend— the weekend of the Yale game. Of the twenty-some young men who were waiting at the station for their dates to arrive on the ten-fifty-two, no more than six or seven were out on the cold, open platform. The rest were standing around in hatless, smoky little groups of twos and threes and fours inside the heated waiting room, talking in voices that, almost without exception, sounded collegiately dogmatic, as though each young man, in his strident, conversational turn, was clearing up, once and for all, some highly controversial issue, one that the outside, non-matriculating world had been bungling, provocatively or not, for centuries.

Lane Coutell, in a Burberry raincoat that apparently had a wool liner buttoned into it, was one of the six or seven boys out on the open platform. Or, rather, he was and he wasn't one of them. For ten minutes or more, he had deliberately been standing just out of conversation range of the other boys, his back against the free Christian Science literature rack, his ungloved hands in his coat pockets. He was wearing a maroon cashmere muffler which had hiked up on his neck, giving him next to no protection against the cold. Abruptly, and rather absently, he took his right hand out of his coat pocket and started to adjust the muffler, but before it was adjusted, he changed his mind and used the same hand to reach inside his coat and take out a letter from the inside pocket of his jacket. He began to read it immediately, with his mouth not quite closed.

The letter was written—typewritten—on pale-blue notepaper. It had a handled, unfresh look, as if it had been taken out of its envelope and read several times before:

Tuesday I think

DEAREST LANE,

I have no idea if you will be able to decipher this as the noise in the dorm is absolutely incredible tonight and I can hardly hear myself think. So if I spell anything wrong kindly have the kindness to overlook it. Incidentally I've taken your advice and resorted to the dictionary a lot lately, so if it cramps my style your to blame. Anyway I just got your beautiful letter and I love you to pieces, distraction, etc., and can hardly wait for the weekend. It's too bad about not being able to get me in Croft House, but I don't actually care where I stay as long as it's warm and no bugs and I see you occasionally, i.e. every single minute. I've been going i.e. crazy lately. I absolutely adore your letter, especially the part about Eliot. I think I'm beginning to look down on all poets except Sappho. I've been reading her like mad, and no vulgar remarks, please. I may even do my term thing on her if I decide to go out for honors and if I can get the moron they assigned me as an advisor to let me. "Delicate Adonis is dying, Cytherea, what shall we do? Beat your breasts, maidens, and rend your tunics." Isn't that *marvellous*? She keeps *doing* that, too. Do you love me? You didn't say once in your horrible letter. I hate you when your being hopelessly super-male and retiscent (sp.?). Not really *hate* you but am constitutionally against strong, silent men. Not that you aren't strong but you know what I mean. It's getting so noisy in here I can hardly hear myself think. Anyway I love you and want to get this off special delivery so you can get it in plenty of time if I can find a stamp in this madhouse. I love you I love you I love you. Do you actually know I've only danced with you *twice* in eleven months? Not counting that time at the Vanguard when you were so tight. I'll probably be hopelessly selfconscious. Incidentally I'll kill you if there's a receiving line at this thing. Till Saturday, my flower!!

All my love,
FRANNY
XXXXXXXX
XXXXXXXX

P.S. Daddy got his X-rays back from the hospital and we're all so relieved. Its a growth but it isn't malignent. I spoke to Mother on the phone last night. Incidentally she sent her regards to you, so you can *relax* about that Friday night. I don't even think they heard us come in.

P.P.S. I sound so unintelligent and dimwitted when I write to you. Why? I give you my permission to analyze it. Let's just try to have a marvellous time this weekend. I mean not try to analyze everything to death for once, if possible, especially me. I love you.

FRANCES (her mark)

Lane was about halfway through this particular reading of the letter when he was interrupted —intruded upon, trespassed upon—by a burly-set young man named Ray Sorenson, who wanted to know if Lane knew what this bastard Rilke was all about. Lane and Sorenson were both in Modern European Literature 251 (open to seniors and graduate students only) and had been assigned the Fourth of Rilke's "Duino Elegies" for Monday. Lane, who knew Sorenson only slightly but had a vague, categorical aversion to his face and manner, put away his letter and said that he didn't know but that he thought he'd understood most of it. "You're lucky," Sorenson said. "You're a fortunate man." His voice carried with a minimum of vitality, as though he had come over to speak to Lane out of boredom or restiveness, not for any sort of human discourse. "Christ, it's cold," he said, and took a pack of cigarettes out of his pocket. Lane noticed a faded but distracting enough lipstick streak on the lapel of Sorenson's camel's-hair coat. It looked as though it had been there for weeks, maybe months, but he didn't know Sorenson well enough to mention it, nor, for that matter, did he give a damn. Besides, the train was arriving. Both boys turned a sort of half left to face the incoming engine. Almost at the same time, the door to the waiting room banged open, and the boys who had been keeping themselves warm began to come out to meet the train, most of them giving the impression of having at least three lighted cigarettes in each hand.

Lane himself lit a cigarette as the train pulled in. Then, like so many people, who, perhaps, ought to be issued only a very probational pass to meet trains, he tried to empty his face of all expression that might quite simply, perhaps even beautifully, reveal how he felt about the arriving person.

Franny was among the first of the girls to get off the train, from a car at the far, northern end of the platform. Lane spotted her immediately, and despite whatever it was he was trying to do with his face, his arm that shot up into the air was the whole truth. Franny saw it, and him, and waved extravagantly back. She was wearing a sheared-raccoon coat, and Lane, walking toward her quickly but with a slow face, reasoned to himself, with suppressed excitement, that he was the only one on the platform who really *knew* Franny's coat. He remembered that once, in a borrowed car, after kissing Franny for a half hour or so, he had kissed her coat lapel, as though it were a perfectly desirable, organic extension of the person herself.

"Lane!" Franny greeted him pleasurably—and she was not one for emptying her face of expression. She threw her arms around him and kissed him. It was a station-platform kiss—spontaneous enough to begin with, but rather inhibited in the follow-through, and with somewhat of a forehead-bumping aspect. "Did you get my letter?" she asked, and added, almost in the same breath, "You look almost frozen, you poor man. Why didn't you wait inside? Did you get my letter?"

"Which letter?" Lane said, picking up her suitcase. It was navy blue with white leather binding, like half a dozen other suitcases that had just been carried off the train.

"You didn't *get* it? I mailed it *Wednesday*. Oh, God! I even took it down to the post—"

"Oh, that one. Yes. This all the bags you brought? What's the book?"

Franny looked down at her left hand. She had a small pea-green clothbound book in it. "This? Oh, just something," she said. She opened her handbag and stuffed the book into it, and followed Lane down the long platform toward the taxi stand. She put her arm through his, and did most of the talking, if not all of it. There was something, first, about a dress in her bag that had to be ironed. She said she'd bought a really darling little iron that looked like it went with a doll house, but had forgotten to bring it. She said she didn't think she'd known more than three girls on the train—Martha Farrar, Tippie Tibbett, and Eleanor somebody, whom she'd met years ago, in her boarding-school days, at Exeter or someplace. Everybody else on the train, Franny said, looked very Smith, except for two absolutely Vassar types and one abso*lute*ly Bennington or Sarah Lawrence type. The Bennington-Sarah Lawrence type looked like she'd spent the whole train ride in the john, sculpting or painting or something, or as though she had a leotard on under her dress. Lane, walking rather too fast, said he was sorry he hadn't been able to get her into Croft House—that was hopeless, of course—but that he'd got her into this very nice, cozy place. Small, but clean and all that. She'd like it, he said, and Franny immediately had a vision of a white clapboard rooming house. Three girls who didn't know each other in one room. Whoever got there first would get the lumpy day bed to herself, and the other two would share a double bed with an absolutely fantastic mattress. "Lovely," she said with enthusiasm. Sometimes it was hell to conceal her impatience over the male of the species' general ineptness, and Lane's in particular. It reminded her of a rainy night in New York, just after theatre, when Lane, with a suspicious excess of curbside charity, had let that really horrible man in the dinner jacket take that taxi away from him. She hadn't especially minded that—that is, *God,* it would be awful to have to be a man and have to get taxis in the rain—but she remembered Lane's really horrible, hostile look at her as he reported back to the curb. Now, feeling oddly guilty as she thought about that and other things, she gave Lane's arm a special little pressure of simulated affection. The two of them got into a cab. The navy-blue bag with the white leather binding went up front with the driver.

"We'll drop your bag and stuff where you're staying—just chuck them in the door—and then we'll go get some lunch," Lane said. "I'm starved." He leaned forward and gave an address to the driver.

"Oh, it's lovely to see you!" Franny said as the cab moved off. "I've *missed* you." The words were no sooner out than she realized that she didn't mean them at all. Again with guilt, she took Lane's hand and tightly, warmly laced fingers with him.

ABOUT an hour later, the two were sitting at a comparatively isolated table in a restaurant called Sickler's, downtown, a highly favored place among, chiefly, the intellectual fringe of students at the college—the same students, more or less, who, had they been Yale or Harvard men, might rather too casually have steered their dates away from Mory's or Cronin's. Sickler's, it might be said, was the only restaurant in town where the steaks weren't "*that* thick"— thumb and index finger held an inch apart. Sickler's was Snails. Sickler's was where a student and his date either both ordered salad or, usually, neither of them did, because of the garlic seasoning. Franny and Lane were both having Martinis. When the drinks had first been served to them, ten or fifteen minutes earlier,

Lane had sampled his, then sat back and briefly looked around the room with an almost palpable sense of well-being at finding himself (he must have been sure no one could dispute) in the right place with an unimpeachably right-looking girl—a girl who was not only extraordinarily pretty but, so much the better, not too categorically cashmere sweater and flannel skirt. Franny had seen this momentary little exposure, and had taken it in for what it was, neither more nor less. But by some old, standing arrangement with her psyche, she elected to feel guilty for having seen it, caught it, and sentenced herself to listen to Lane's ensuing conversation with a special semblance of absorption.

Lane was speaking now as someone does who has been monopolizing conversation for a good quarter of an hour or so and who believes he has just hit a stride where his voice can do absolutely no wrong. "I mean, to put it crudely," he was saying, "the thing you could say he lacks is testicularity. Know what I mean?" He was slouched rhetorically forward, toward Franny, his receptive audience, a supporting forearm on either side of his Martini.

"Lacks what?" Franny said. She had had to clear her throat before speaking, it had been so long since she had said anything at all.

Lane hesitated. "Masculinity," he said.

"I heard you the first time."

"Anyway, that was the motif of the thing, so to speak—what I was trying to bring out in a fairly subtle way," Lane said, very closely following the trend of his own conversation. "I mean, *God*. I honestly thought it was going to go over like a goddam lead balloon, and when I got it back with this goddam '*A*' on it in letters about six feet high, I swear I nearly keeled over."

Franny again cleared her throat. Apparently her self-imposed sentence of unadulterated good-listenership had been fully served. "Why?" she asked.

Lane looked faintly interrupted. "Why what?"

"Why'd you think it was going to go over like a lead balloon?"

"I just told you. I just got through saying. This guy Brughman is a big Flaubert man. Or at least I thought he was."

"Oh," Franny said. She smiled. She sipped her Martini. "This is marvellous," she said, looking at the glass. "I'm so glad it's not about twenty to one. I hate it when they're absolutely all gin."

Lane nodded. "Anyway, I think I've got the goddam paper in my room. If we get a chance over the weekend, I'll read it to you."

"Marvellous. I'd love to hear it."

Lane nodded again. "I mean I didn't say anything too goddam world-shaking or anything like that." He shifted his position in the chair. "But—I don't know—I think the emphasis I put on *why* he was so neurotically attracted to the *mot juste* wasn't too bad. I mean in the light of what we know today. Not just psychoanalysis and all that crap, but certainly to a certain extent. You know what I mean. I'm no Freudian man or anything like that, but certain things you can't just pass over as capital-F Freudian and let them go at that. I mean to a certain extent I think I was perfectly justified to point out that none of the really good boys—Tolstoy, Dostoevski, *Shake*speare, for Chrissake—were such goddam word-squeezers. They just *wrote*. Know what I mean?" Lane looked at Franny somewhat expectantly. She seemed to him to have been listening with extra-special intentness.

"You going to eat your olive, or what?"

Lane gave his Martini glass a brief glance, then looked back at Franny. "No," he said coldly. "You want it?"

"If you don't," Franny said. She knew from Lane's expression that she had asked the wrong question. What was worse, she suddenly didn't want the olive at all and wondered why she had even *asked* for it. There was nothing to do, though, when Lane extended his Martini glass to her but to accept the olive and consume it with apparent relish. She then took a cigarette from Lane's pack on the table, and he lit it for her and one for himself.

After the interruption of the olive, a short silence came over the table. When Lane broke it, it was because he was not one to keep a punch line to himself for any length of time. "This guy Brughman thinks I ought to publish the goddam paper somewhere," he said abruptly. "I don't know, though." Then, as though he had suddenly become exhausted — or, rather, depleted by the demands made on him by a world greedy for the fruit of his intellect—he began to massage the side of his face with the flat of his hand, removing, with unconscious crassness, a bit of sleep from one eye. "I mean critical essays on Flaubert and those boys are a goddam dime a dozen." He reflected, looking a trifle morose. "As a matter of fact, I don't think there've been any really in*cis*ive jobs done on him in the last—"

"You're talking like a section man. But exactly."

"I beg your pardon?" Lane said with measured quietness.

"You're talking exactly like a section man. I'm sorry, but you are. You really are."

"I am? How does a section man talk, may I ask?"

Franny saw that he was irritated, and to what extent, but, for the moment, with equal parts of self-disapproval and malice, she felt like speaking her mind. "Well, I don't know what they are around here, but where *I* come from, a section man's a person that takes over a class when the professor isn't there or is busy having a nervous breakdown or is at the dentist or something. He's usually a graduate student or something. Anyway, if it's a course in Russian Literature, say, he comes in, in his little button-down-collar shirt and striped tie, and starts knocking Turgenev for about a half hour. Then, when he's finished, when he's completely *ruined* Turgenev for you, he starts talking about Stendhal or somebody he wrote his thesis for his M.A. on. Where I go, the English Department has about ten little section men running around ruining things for people, and they're all so brilliant they can hardly open their mouths—pardon the contradiction. I mean if you get into an argument with them, all they do is get this terribly *benign* expression on their—"

"You've got a goddam bug today—you know that? What the hell's the matter with you anyway?"

Franny quickly tipped her cigarette ash, then brought the ashtray an inch closer to her side of the table. "I'm sorry. I'm awful," she said. "I've just felt so *destructive* all week. It's awful. I'm horrible."

"Your letter didn't sound so goddam destructive."

Franny nodded solemnly. She was looking at a little warm blotch of sunshine, about the size of a poker chip, on the tablecloth. "I had to strain to write it," she said.

Lane started to say something to that, but the waiter was suddenly there to take away the empty Martini glasses. "You want another one?" Lane asked Franny.

He didn't get an answer. Franny was staring at the little blotch of sunshine with a special intensity, as if she were considering lying down in it.

"Franny," Lane said patiently, for the waiter's benefit. "Would you like another Martini, or what?"

She looked up. "I'm sorry." She looked at the removed, empty glasses in the waiter's hand. "No. Yes. I don't know."

Lane gave a laugh, looking at the waiter. "Which is it?" he said.

"Yes, please." She looked more alert.

The waiter left. Lane watched him leave the room, then looked back at Franny. She was shaping her cigarette ash on the side of the fresh ashtray the waiter had brought, her mouth not quite closed. Lane watched her for a moment with mounting irritation. Quite probably, he resented and feared any signs of detachment in a girl he was seriously dating. In any case, he surely was concerned over the possibility that this bug Franny had might bitch up the whole weekend. He suddenly leaned forward, putting his arms on the table, as though to get this thing ironed out, by God, but Franny spoke up before he did. "I'm lousy today," she said. "I'm just way off today." She found herself looking at Lane as if he were a stranger, or a poster advertising a brand of linoleum, across the aisle of a subway car. Again she felt the trickle of disloyalty and guilt, which seemed to be the order of the day, and reacted to it by reaching over to cover Lane's hand with her own. She withdrew her hand almost immediately and used it to pick her cigarette out of the ashtray. "I'll snap out of this in a minute," she said. "I absolutely promise." She smiled at Lane—in a sense, genuinely —and at that moment a smile in return might at least have mitigated to some small extent certain events that were to follow, but Lane was busy affecting a brand of detachment of his own, and chose not to smile back. Franny dragged on her cigarette. "If it weren't so late and everything," she said, "and if I hadn't decided like a fool to go out for *honors,* I think I'd drop English. I don't know." She tipped her ashes. "I'm just so sick of pedants and conceited little tearer-downers I could scream." She looked at Lane. "I'm sorry. I'll stop. I give you my word. . . . It's just that if I'd had any guts at all, I wouldn't have gone back to college at all this year. I don't know. I mean it's all the most incredible farce."

"Brilliant. That's really brilliant."

Franny took the sarcasm as her due. "I'm sorry," she said.

"Stop saying you're sorry—do you mind? I don't suppose it's occurred to you that you're making one *hell*uva sweeping generalization. If all English Department people were such great little tearer-downers, it would be an altogether different—"

Franny interrupted him, but almost inaudibly. She was looking over his charcoal flannel shoulder at some abstraction across the dining room.

"What?" Lane asked.

"I said I know. You're right. I'm just off, that's all. Don't pay any attention to me."

But Lane couldn't let a controversy drop until it had been resolved in his favor. "I mean, hell," he said. "There are incompetent people in all walks of life. I mean that's basic. Let's drop the goddam section men for a minute." He looked at Franny. "You listening to me, or what?"

"Yes."

"You've got two of the best men in the country in your goddam English Department. Manlius. Esposito. God, I wish we had them *here*. At least, they're poets, for Chrissake."

"They're not," Franny said. "That's partly what's so awful. I mean they're not *real* poets. They're just people that write poems that get published and anthologized all over the place, but they're not *poets*." She stopped, self-consciously, and put out her cigarette. For several minutes now, she had seemed to be losing color in her face. Suddenly, even her lipstick seemed a shade or two lighter, as though she had just blotted it with a leaf of Kleenex. "Let's not talk about it," she said, almost listlessly, squashing her cigarette stub in the ashtray. "I'm way off. I'll just ruin the whole weekend. Maybe there's a trapdoor under my chair, and I'll just disappear."

The waiter came forward very briefly, and left a second Martini in front of each of them.

Lane put his fingers—which were slender and long, and usually not far out of sight—around the stem of his glass. "You're not *ruin*ing anything," he said quietly. "I'm just interested in finding out what the hell goes. I mean do you have to be a goddam bohemian type, or *dead*, for Chrissake, to be a *real poet*? What do you want—some bastard with wavy hair?"

"No. Can't we let it go? Please. I'm feeling absolutely lousy, and I'm getting a terrible—"

"I'd be very happy to drop the whole subject —I'd be delighted. Just tell me first what a *real poet* is, if you don't mind. I'd appreciate it. I really would."

There was a faint glisten of perspiration high on Franny's forehead. It might only have meant that the room was too warm, or that her stomach was upset, or that the Martinis were too potent; in any case, Lane didn't seem to notice it.

"I don't *know* what a real poet is. I wish you'd *stop* it, Lane. I'm serious. I'm feeling very peculiar and funny, and I can't—"

"All right, all right—O.K. Relax," Lane said. "I was only trying—"

"I know this much, is all," Franny said. "If you're a poet, you do something beautiful. I mean you're supposed to *leave* something beautiful after you get off the page and everything. The ones you're talking about don't leave a single, solitary thing beautiful. All that maybe the slightly better ones do is sort of get inside your head and leave *some*thing there, but just because they *do*, just because they know how to leave *some*thing, it doesn't have to be a *poem*, for heaven's sake. It may just be some kind of terribly fascinating, syntaxy *droppings*—excuse the expression. Like Manlius and Esposito and all those poor men."

Lane took time to light a cigarette for himself before he said anything. Then: "I thought you liked Manlius. As a matter of fact, about a month ago, if I remember correctly, you said he was *dar*ling, and that you—"

"I do like him. I'm sick of just liking people. I wish to God I could meet somebody I could respect. . . . Would you excuse me for just a minute?" Franny was suddenly on her feet, with her handbag in her hand. She was very pale.

Lane got up, pushing back his chair, his mouth somewhat open. "What's the matter?" he asked. "You feel all right? Anything wrong, or what?"

"I'll be back in just a second."

She left the room without asking directions, as though she knew from former lunches at Sickler's just where to go.

Lane, alone at the table, sat smoking and taking conservative drinks from his Martini to make it last till Franny got back. It was very clear that the sense of well-being he had felt, a half hour earlier, at being in the right place with the right, or right-looking, girl was now totally gone. He looked over at the sheared-rac-coon coat, which lay somewhat askew over the

back of Franny's vacant chair—the same coat
that had excited him at the station, by virtue of
his singular familiarity with it—and he examined it now with all but unqualified disaffec-
tion. The wrinkles in the silk lining seemed, for
some reason, to annoy him. He stopped looking
at it and began to stare at the stem of his Martini glass, looking worried and vaguely, unfairly
conspired against. One thing was sure. The
weekend was certainly getting off to a goddam
peculiar start. At that moment, though, he
chanced to look up from the table and see someone he knew across the room—a classmate, with
a date. Lane sat up a bit in his chair and adjusted his expression from that of all-round ap-
prehension and discontent to that of a man
whose date has merely gone to the john, leaving
him, as dates do, with nothing to do in the
meantime but smoke and look bored, preferably attractively bored.

THE ladies' room at Sickler's was almost as large
as the dining room proper, and, in a special
sense, appeared to be hardly less commodious.
It was unattended and apparently unoccupied
when Franny came in. She stood for a moment
—rather as though it were a rendezvous point
of some kind—in the middle of the tiled floor.
Her brow was beaded with perspiration now,
her mouth was slackly open, and she was still
paler than she had been in the dining room.
  Abruptly, then, and very quickly, she went

into the farthest and most anonymous-looking
of the seven or eight enclosures—which, by luck,
didn't require a coin for entrance—closed the
door behind her, and, with some little difficulty,
manipulated the bolt to a locked position. Without any apparent regard to the suchness of her
environment, she sat down. She brought her
knees together very firmly, as if to make herself
a smaller, more compact unit. Then she placed
her hands, vertically, over her eyes and pressed
the heels hard, as though to paralyze the optic
nerve and drown all images into a voidlike
black. Her extended fingers, though trembling,
or because they were trembling, looked oddly
graceful and pretty. She held that tense, almost
fetal position for a suspensory moment—then
broke down. She cried for fully five minutes.
She cried without trying to suppress any of the
noisier manifestations of grief and confusion,
with all the convulsive throat sounds that a hys-
terical child makes when the breath is trying
to get up through a partly closed epiglottis. And
yet, when finally she stopped, she merely stopped,
without the painful, knifelike intakes of breath
that usually follow a violent outburst-inburst.
When she stopped, it was as though some mo-
mentous change of polarity had taken place inside her mind, one that had an immediate, paci-
fying effect on her body. Her face tear-streaked
but quite expressionless, almost vacuous, she
picked up her handbag from the floor, opened
it, and took out the small pea-green clothbound

book. She put it on her lap—on her knees, rather—and looked down at it, gazed down at it,
as if that were the best of all places for a small
pea-green clothbound book to be. After a moment, she picked up the book, raised it chest-
high, and pressed it to her—firmly, and quite
briefly. Then she put it back into the handbag,
stood up, and came out of the enclosure. She
washed her face with cold water, dried it with
a towel from an overhead rack, applied fresh
lipstick, combed her hair, and left the room.

She looked quite stunning as she walked
across the dining room to the table, not at all
unlike a girl on the *qui vive* appropriate to a big
college weekend. As she came briskly, smiling,
to her chair, Lane slowly got up, a napkin in
his left hand.

"God. I'm sorry," Franny said. "Did you think
I'd died?"

"I didn't think you'd *died*," Lane said. He
drew her chair for her. "I didn't know what the
hell happened." He went around to his own
chair. "We don't have any too goddam much
time, you know." He sat down. "You all right?
Your eyes are a little bloodshot." He looked at
her more closely. "You O.K., or what?"

Franny lit a cigarette. "I'm marvellous *now*. I
just never felt so fantastically *rocky* in my entire life. Did you order?"

"I waited for you," Lane said, still looking at
her closely. "What was the matter anyway? Your
stomach?"

"No. Yes and no. I don't know," Franny said. She looked down at the menu on her plate, and consulted it without picking it up. "All I want's a chicken sandwich. And maybe a glass of milk. . . . You order what you want and all, though. I mean, take snails and octopuses and things. Octopi. I'm really not at all hungry."

Lane looked at her, then exhaled a thin, overly expressive stream of smoke down at his plate. "This is going to be a real little doll of a weekend," he said. "A chicken sandwich, for God's sake."

Franny was annoyed. "I'm not hungry, Lane —I'm *sorry*. My gosh. Now, please. You order what you want, why don't you, and I'll eat while you're eating. But I can't just work up an appetite because you want me to."

"All right, all right." Lane craned his neck and caught the waiter's attention. A moment later, he ordered the chicken sandwich and the glass of milk for Franny, and snails, frogs' legs, and a salad for himself. He looked at his wristwatch when the waiter had gone, and said, "We're supposed to be up at Tenbridge at one-fifteen, one-thirty, incidentally. No later. I told Wally we'd probably stop off for a drink and then maybe we'd all go out to the stadium together in his car. You mind? You like Wally."

"I don't even know who he is."

"You've met him about twenty times, for God's sake. Wally Campbell. Jesus. If you've met him once, you've met him—"

"Oh. I remember. . . . Listen, don't *hate* me because I can't remember some person immediately. Especially when they look like everybody else, and talk and dress and act like everybody else." Franny made her voice stop. It sounded to her cavilling and bitchy, and she felt a wave of self-hatred that, quite literally, made her forehead begin to perspire again. But her voice picked up again, in spite of herself. "I don't mean there's anything horrible about him or anything like that. It's just that for four solid years I've kept seeing Wally Campbells wherever I go. I know when they're going to be *charming,* I know when they're going to start telling you some really nasty gossip about some girl that lives in your dorm, I know when they're going to ask me what I did over the summer, I know when they're going to pull up a chair and straddle it backward and start bragging in a terribly, terribly quiet voice—or *name*-dropping in a terribly quiet, *casual* voice. There's an unwritten law that people in a certain social or financial bracket can name-drop as much as they like just as long as they say something terribly disparaging about the person as soon as they've dropped his name—that he's a bastard or a nymphomaniac or takes dope all the time, or *some*thing horrible." She broke off again. She was quiet for a moment, turning the ashtray in her fingers and being careful not to look up and see Lane's expression. "I'm sorry," she said. "It isn't just Wally Campbell. I'm just picking on him because you mentioned him. And because he just looks like somebody that spent the summer in Italy or someplace."

"He was in France last summer, for your information," Lane stated. "I know what you mean," he added quickly, "but you're being goddam un—"

"All right," Franny said wearily. "France." She took a cigarette out of the pack on the table. "It isn't just Wally. It could be a girl, for goodness' sake. I mean if he were a girl—somebody in my dorm, for example—he'd have been painting scenery in some stock company all summer. Or bicycled through Wales. Or taken an apartment in New York and worked for a magazine or an advertising company. It's *every*body, I mean. Everything everybody does is so—I don't know—not *wrong,* or even mean, or even stupid necessarily. But just so tiny and meaningless and—sad-making. And the worst part is, if you go bohemian or something crazy like that, you're conforming just as much as everybody else, only in a different way." She stopped. She shook her head briefly, her face quite white, and for just a fractional moment she felt her forehead with her hand—less, it seemed, to find out whether she was perspiring than to check to see, as if she were her own parent, whether she had a fever. "I feel so funny," she said. "I think I'm going crazy. Maybe I'm already crazy."

Lane was looking at her with genuine concern—more concern than curiosity. "You're pale as hell. You're really pale—you know that?" he asked.

Franny shook her head. "I'm fine. I'll be fine in a minute." She looked up as the waiter came forward with their orders. "Oh, your snails look beautiful." She had just brought her cigarette to her lips, but it had gone out. "What'd you do with the matches?" she asked.

Lane gave her a light when the waiter had gone. "You smoke too much," he said. He picked up the small fork beside his plate of snails, but looked at Franny again before he used it. "I'm worried about you. I'm serious. What the hell's happened to you in the last couple of weeks?"

Franny looked at him, then simultaneously shrugged and shook her head. "Nothing. Absolutely nothing," she said. "Eat. Eat them snails. They're terrible if they're cold."

"*You* eat."

Franny nodded and looked down at her chicken sandwich. She felt a faint wave of nausea, and looked up immediately and dragged on her cigarette.

"How's the play?" Lane asked, attending to his snails.

"I don't know. I'm not in it. I quit."

"You quit?" Lane looked up. "I thought you were so mad about the part. What happened? They give it to somebody else?"

"No, they did not. It was all mine. That's nasty. Oh, that's nasty."

"Well, what happened? You didn't quit the whole department, did you?"

Franny nodded, and took a sip of her milk.

Lane waited till he had chewed and swallowed, then said, "Why, for God's sake? I thought the goddam theatre was your passion. It's about the only thing I've ever heard you—"

"I just quit, that's all," Franny said. "It started embarrassing me. I began to feel like such a nasty little egomaniac." She reflected. "I don't know. It seemed like such poor taste, sort of, to want to act in the first place. I mean all the *ego*. And I used to hate myself so, when I was in a play, to be backstage after the play was over. All those egos running around feeling terribly *charitable* and *warm*. Kissing everybody and wearing their makeup all over the place, and then trying to be horribly natural and friendly when your friends came backstage to see you. I just hated myself. . . . And the worst part was I was usually sort of ashamed to be in the plays I was in. Especially in summer stock." She looked at Lane. "And I had good parts, so don't look at me that way. It wasn't that. It was just that I would've been ashamed if, say, anybody I respected—my brothers, for example—came and heard me deliver some of the *lines* I had to say. I used to write certain people and tell them not to come." She reflected again. "Except Pegeen in 'Playboy,' last summer. I mean that could have been really nice, only the goon that played the

Playboy spoiled any fun it might have been. He was so lyrical—God, was he lyrical!"

Lane had finished his snails. He sat looking deliberately expressionless. "He got terrific reviews," he said. "You sent me the reviews, if you recall."

Franny sighed. "All right. O.K., Lane."

"No, I mean you've been talking for a half hour as though you're the only person in the world that's got any goddam sense, any critical ability. I mean if some of the best critics thought this man was terrific in the play, maybe he was, maybe you're wrong. That ever occur to you? You know, you haven't exactly reached the ripe, old—"

"He was terrific for somebody that just has talent. If you're going to play the Playboy right, you have to be a genius. You *do*, that's all—I can't help it," Franny said. She arched her back a trifle, and, with her mouth a trifle open, she put her hand on top of her head. "I feel so woozy and funny. I don't know what's the matter with me."

"You think *you're* a genius?"

Franny took her hand down from her head. "Aw, Lane. Please. Don't do that to me."

"I'm not doing any—"

"All I know is I'm losing my mind," Franny said. "I'm just sick of ego, ego, ego. My own and everybody else's. I'm sick of everybody that wants to *get* somewhere, do something distinguished

and all, be somebody interesting. It's disgusting
—it is, it *is*. I don't care what anybody says."

Lane raised his eyebrows at that, and sat back,
the better to make his point. "You sure you're
just not afraid of competing?" he asked with
studied quietness. "I don't know too much about
it, but I'd lay odds a good psychoanalyst—I mean
a really competent one—would probably take
that statement—"

"I'm not afraid to compete. It's just the opposite. Don't you see that? I'm afraid I *will*
compete—that's what scares me. That's why I
quit the Theatre Department. Just because I'm
so horribly conditioned to accept everybody
else's values, and just because I like applause
and people to rave about me, doesn't make it
right. I'm ashamed of it. I'm sick of it. I'm sick
of not having the courage to be an absolute nobody. I'm sick of myself and everybody else
that wants to make some kind of a splash." She
paused, and suddenly picked up her glass of
milk and brought it to her lips. "I knew it," she
said, setting it down. "That's something new.
My teeth go funny on me. They're chattering. I
nearly bit through a glass the day before yesterday. Maybe I'm stark, staring mad and don't
know it." The waiter had come forward to serve
Lane's frogs' legs and salad, and Franny looked
up at him. He, in turn, looked down at her untouched chicken sandwich. He asked if the
young lady would perhaps like to change her
order. Franny thanked him, and said no. "I'm

just very slow," she said. The waiter, who was not a young man, seemed to look for an instant at her pallor and damp brow, then bowed and left.

"You want to use this a second?" Lane said abruptly. He was holding out a folded, white handkerchief. His voice sounded sympathetic, kind, in spite of some perverse attempt to make it sound matter-of-fact.

"Why? Do I need it?"

"You're sweating. Not sweating, but I mean your forehead's perspiring quite a bit."

"It *is*? How horrible! I'm sorry. . . ." Franny brought her handbag up to table level, opened it, and began to rummage through it. "I have some Kleenex somewhere."

"Use my handkerchief, for God's sake. What the hell's the difference?"

"*No*—I love that handkerchief and I'm not going to get it all perspiry," Franny said. Her handbag was a crowded one. To see better, she began to unload a few things and place them on the tablecloth, just to the left of her untasted sandwich. "Here it is," she said. She used a compact mirror and quickly, lightly blotted her brow with a leaf of Kleenex. "God. I look like a ghost. How can you stand me?"

"What's the book?" Lane asked.

FRANNY literally jumped. She looked down at the disorderly little pile of handbag freight on the tablecloth. "What book?" she said. "This, you mean?" She picked up the little clothbound book and put it back into her handbag. "Just something I brought to look at on the train."

"Let's have a look. What is it?"

Franny didn't seem to hear him. She opened her compact again and took another quick glance into the mirror. "God," she said. Then she cleared everything—compact, billfold, laundry bill, toothbrush, a tin of aspirins, and a gold-plated swizzle stick—back into her handbag. "I don't know why I carry that crazy gold swizzle stick around," she said. "A very corny boy gave it to me when I was a sophomore, for my birthday. He thought it was such a beautiful and inspired gift, and he kept watching my face while I opened the package. I keep trying to throw it away, but I simply can't do it. I'll go to my grave with it." She reflected. "He kept grinning at me and telling me I'd always have good luck if I kept it with me at all times."

Lane had started in on his frogs' legs. "What was the book, anyway? Or is it a goddam secret or something?" he asked.

"The little book in my bag?" Franny said. She watched him disjoint a pair of frogs' legs. Then she took a cigarette from the pack on the table and lit it herself. "Oh, I don't know," she said. "It's something called 'The Way of a Pilgrim.'" She watched Lane eat for a moment. "I got it out of the library. This man that teaches this Religion Survey thing I'm taking this term mentioned it." She dragged on her cigarette.

"I've had it out for weeks. I keep forgetting to return it."

"Who wrote it?"

"I don't know," Franny said casually. "Some Russian peasant, apparently." She went on watching Lane eat his frogs' legs. "He never gives his name. You never know his name the whole time he's telling the story. He just tells you he's a peasant and that he's thirty-three years old and that he's got a withered arm. And that his wife is dead. It's all in the eighteen-hundreds."

Lane had just shifted his attention from the frogs' legs to the salad. "Any good?" he said. "What's it about?"

"I don't know. It's peculiar. I mean it's primarily a religious book. In a way, I suppose you could say it's terribly fanatical, but in a way it isn't. I mean it starts out with this peasant—the pilgrim—wanting to find out what it means in the Bible when it says you should pray incessantly. You know. Without stopping. In Thessalonians or someplace. So he starts out walking all over Russia, looking for somebody who can tell him *how* to pray incessantly. And what you should say if you do." Franny seemed intensely interested in the way Lane was dismembering his frogs' legs. Her eyes remained fixed on his plate as she spoke. "All he carries with him is this knapsack filled with bread and salt. Then he meets this person called a starets—some sort of terribly advanced religious person—and the starets tells him about a book called the 'Philokalia.' Which apparently was written by a group of terribly advanced monks who sort of advocated this really incredible method of praying."

"Hold still," Lane said to a pair of frogs' legs.

"Anyway, so the pilgrim learns how to pray the way these very mystical persons say you should—I mean he keeps at it till he's perfected it and everything. Then he goes on walking all over Russia, meeting all kinds of absolutely marvellous people and telling them how to pray by this incredible method. I mean that's really the whole book."

"I hate to mention it, but I'm going to reek of garlic," Lane said.

"He meets this one married couple, on one of his journeys, that I love more than anybody I ever read about in my entire life," Franny said. "He's walking down a road somewhere in the country, with his knapsack on his back, when these two tiny little children run after him, shouting, 'Dear little beggar! Dear little beggar! You must come home to Mummy. She likes beggars.' So he goes home with the children, and this *really* lovely person, the children's mother, comes out of the house all in a bustle and insists on helping him take off his dirty old boots and giving him a cup of tea. Then the father comes home, and apparently he loves beggars and pilgrims, too, and they all sit down to dinner. And while they're at dinner, the pilgrim wants to know who all the ladies are that are sitting around the table, and the husband tells him that they're all servants but that they always sit down to eat with him and his wife because they're sisters in Christ." Franny suddenly sat up a trifle straighter in her seat, self-consciously. "I mean I loved the pilgrim wanting to know who all the ladies were." She watched Lane butter a piece of bread. "Anyway, after that, the pilgrim stays overnight, and he and the husband sit up till late talking about this method of praying without ceasing. The pilgrim tells him how to do it. Then he leaves in the morning and starts out on some more adventures. He meets all kinds of people—I mean that's the whole book, really—and he tells all of them how to pray by this special way."

Lane nodded. He cut into his salad with his fork. "I hope to God we get time over the weekend so that you can take a quick look at this goddam paper I told you about," he said. "I don't know. I may not do a damn thing with it —I mean try to publish it or what have you— but I'd like you to sort of glance through it while you're here."

"I'd love to," Franny said. She watched him butter another piece of bread. "You might like this book," she said suddenly. "It's so simple, I mean."

"Sounds interesting. You don't want your butter, do you?"

"No, take it. I can't lend it to you, because it's way overdue already, but you could probably get it at the library here. I'm positive you could."

"You haven't touched your goddam sandwich," Lane said suddenly. "You know that?"

Franny looked down at her plate as if it had just been placed before her. "I will in a minute," she said. She sat still for a moment, holding her cigarette, but without dragging on it, in her left hand, and with her right hand fixed tensely around the base of the glass of milk. "Do you want to hear what the special method of praying was that the starets told him about?" she asked. "It's really sort of interesting, in a way."

Lane cut into his last pair of frogs' legs. He nodded. "Sure," he said. "Sure."

"Well, as I said, the pilgrim—this simple peasant—started the whole pilgrimage to find out what it means in the Bible when it says you're supposed to pray without ceasing. And then he meets this starets—this very advanced religious person I mentioned, the one who'd been studying the 'Philokalia' for years and years and years." Franny stopped suddenly to reflect, to organize. "Well, the starets tells him about the Jesus Prayer first of all. 'Lord Jesus Christ, have mercy on me.' I mean that's what it is. And he explains to him that those are the best words to use when you pray. Especially the word 'mercy,' because it's such a really enormous word and can mean so many things. I mean it doesn't just have to mean *mercy*." Franny paused to reflect again. She was no longer looking at Lane's plate but over his shoulder. "Any-

way," she went on, "the starets tells the pilgrim
that if you keep saying that prayer over and
over again—you only have to just do it with
your *lips* at first—then eventually what happens, the prayer becomes self-active. Something
happens after a while. I don't know what, but
something happens, and the words get synchro-
nized with the person's heartbeats, and then
you're actually praying without ceasing. Which
has a really tremendous, mystical effect on your
whole outlook. I mean that's the whole *point* of
it, more or less. I mean you do it to purify your
whole outlook and get an absolutely new conception of what everything's about."

Lane had finished eating. Now, as Franny
paused again, he sat back and lit a cigarette and
watched her face. She was still looking abstractedly ahead of her, past his shoulder, and seemed
scarcely aware of his presence.

"But the thing is, the marvellous thing is,
when you first start doing it, you don't even
have to have *faith* in what you're doing. I mean
even if you're terribly embarrassed about the
whole thing, it's perfectly all right. I mean you're
not *insult*ing anybody or anything. In other
words, nobody asks you to believe a single thing
when you first start out. You don't even have to
think about what you're saying, the starets said.
All you have to have in the beginning is quantity. Then, later on, it becomes quality by itself.
On its own power or something. He says that
any name of God—any name at all—has this pe-

culiar, self-active power of its own, and it starts working after you've sort of started it up."

Lane sat rather slouched in his chair, smoking, his eyes narrowed attentively at Franny's face. Her face was still pale, but it had been paler at other moments since the two had been in Sickler's.

"As a matter of fact, that makes absolute sense," Franny said, "because in the Nembutsu sects of Buddhism, people keep saying 'Namu Amida Butsu' over and over again—which means 'Praises to the Buddha' or something like that— and the *same thing* happens. The exact same—"

"Easy. Take it easy," Lane interrupted. "In the first place, you're going to burn your fingers any second."

Franny gave a minimal glance down at her left hand, and dropped the stub of her still-burning cigarette into the ashtray. "The same thing happens in 'The Cloud of Unknowing,' too. Just with the word 'God.' I mean you just keep saying the word 'God.' " She looked at Lane more directly than she had in several minutes. "I mean the point is did you ever hear anything so fascinating in your *life,* in a way? I mean it's so hard to just say it's absolute co*in*cidence and then just let it go at that—that's what's so fascinating to me. At least, that's what's so terribly—" She broke off. Lane was shifting restively in his chair, and there was an expression on his face—a matter of raised eyebrows, chiefly—that she knew very well. "What's the matter?" she asked.

"You actually believe that stuff, or what?"

Franny reached for the pack of cigarettes and took one out. "I didn't say I believed it or I didn't believe it," she said, and scanned the table for the folder of matches. "I said it was fascinating." She accepted a light from Lane. "I just think it's a terribly peculiar coincidence," she said, exhaling smoke, "that you keep running into that kind of advice— I mean all these really advanced and absolutely unbogus religious persons that keep telling you if you repeat the name of God incessantly, something *happens*. Even in India. In India, they tell you to meditate on the 'Om,' which means the same thing, really, and the exact same result is supposed to happen. So I mean you can't just rationalize it away without even—"

"What *is* the result?" Lane said shortly.

"What?"

"I mean what *is* the result that's supposed to follow? All this synchronization business and mumbo-jumbo. You get heart trouble? I don't know if you know it, but you could do yourself, somebody could do himself a great deal of real—"

"You get to see God. Something happens in some absolutely nonphysical part of the heart— where the Hindus say that Atman resides, if you ever took any Religion—and you see God, that's all." She flicked her cigarette ash self-consciously, just missing the ashtray. She picked up the ash with her fingers and put it in. "And don't ask me who or what God is. I mean I don't even know if He exists. When I was little, I used to think—" She stopped. The waiter had come to take away the dishes and redistribute menus.

"You want some dessert, or coffee?" Lane asked.

"I think I'll just finish my milk. But you have some," Franny said. The waiter had just taken away her plate with the untouched chicken sandwich. She didn't dare to look up at him.

Lane looked at his wristwatch. "God. We don't have time. We're lucky if we get to the *game* on time." He looked up at the waiter. "Just coffee for me, please." He watched the waiter leave, then leaned forward, arms on the table, thoroughly relaxed, stomach full, coffee due to arrive momentarily, and said, "Well, it's interesting, anyway. All that stuff . . . I don't think you leave any margin for the most elementary psy*chol*ogy. I mean I think all those religious experiences have a very obvious psychological background—you know what I mean. . . . It's interesting, though. I mean you can't deny that." He looked over at Franny and smiled at her. "Anyway. Just in case I forgot to mention it. I love you. Did I get around to mentioning that?"

"Lane, would you excuse me again for just a

second?" Franny said. She had got up before the question was completely out.

Lane got up, too, slowly, looking at her. "You all right?" he asked. "You feel sick again, or what?"

"Just funny. I'll be right back."

She walked briskly through the dining room, taking the same route she had taken earlier. But she stopped quite short at the small cocktail bar at the far end of the room. The bartender, who was wiping a sherry glass dry, looked at her. She put her right hand on the bar, then lowered her head—bowed it—and put her left hand to her forehead, just touching it with the fingertips. She weaved a trifle, then fainted, collapsing to the floor.

IT was nearly five minutes before Franny came thoroughly to. She was on a couch in the manager's office, and Lane was sitting beside her. His face, suspended anxiously over hers, had a remarkable pallor of its own now.

"How are ya?" he said, in a rather hospital-room voice. "You feel any better?"

Franny nodded. She closed her eyes for a second against the overhead light, then reopened them. "Am I supposed to say 'Where am I?'" she said. "Where am I?"

Lane laughed. "You're in the manager's office. They're all running around looking for spirits of ammonia and doctors and things to bring you to. They'd just run out of ammonia, apparently. How do you feel? No kidding."

"Fine. *Stupid,* but fine. Did I honestly *faint?*"

"And how. You really conked out," Lane said. He took her hand in his. "What do you think's the matter with you anyway? I mean you sounded so—you know—so perfect when I talked to you on the phone last week. Didn't you eat any breakfast, or what?"

Franny shrugged. Her eyes looked around the room. "It's so embarrassing," she said. "Did somebody have to *carry* me in here?"

"The bartender and I. We sort of hoisted you in. You scared the hell out of me, I'm not kidding."

Franny looked thoughtfully, without blinking, at the ceiling while her hand was held. Then she turned and, with her free hand, made a gesture as though to push back the cuff of Lane's sleeve. "What time is it?" she asked.

"Never mind that," Lane said. "We're in no hurry."

"You wanted to go to that cocktail party."

"The hell with it."

"Is it too late for the game, too?" Franny asked.

"Listen, I said the hell with it. You're going to go back to your room at whosis—Blue Shutters—and get some rest, that's the important thing," Lane said. He sat a trifle closer to her and bent down and kissed her, briefly. He turned and looked over at the door, then back at Franny. "You're just going to *rest* this afternoon. That's all you're going to do." He stroked her arm for a moment. "Then maybe after a while, if you get any decent rest, I can get upstairs somehow. I think there's a goddam back staircase. I can find out."

Franny didn't say anything. She looked at the ceiling.

"You know how long it's been?" Lane said. "When was that Friday night? Way the hell early last month, wasn't it?" He shook his head. "That's no good. Too goddam long between drinks. To put it crassly." He looked down at Franny more closely. "You really feel better?"

She nodded. She turned her head toward him. "I'm terribly thirsty, that's all. Do you think I could have some water? Would it be too much trouble?"

"Hell, no! Will you be all right if I leave you for a second? You know what I think I'll do?"

Franny shook her head to the second question.

"I'll get somebody to bring you some water. Then I'll get the headwaiter and call off the spirits of ammonia—and, incidentally, pay the check. Then I'll get a cab all ready, so we won't have to hunt all around for one. It may take a few minutes, because most of them will be cruising around for people going out to the game." He let go Franny's hand and got up. "O.K.?" he said.

"Fine."

"O.K., I'll be right back. Don't move." He left the room.

Alone, Franny lay quite still, looking at the ceiling. Her lips began to move, forming soundless words, and they continued to move.

Zooey

THE facts at hand presumably speak for themselves, but a trifle more vulgarly, I suspect, than facts even usually do. As a counterbalance, then, we begin with that everfresh and exciting odium: the author's formal introduction. The one I have in mind not only is wordy and earnest beyond my wildest dreams but is, to boot, rather excruciatingly personal. If, with the right kind of luck, it comes off, it should be comparable in effect to a compulsory guided tour through the engine room, with myself, as guide, leading the way in an old one-piece Jantzen bathing suit.

To get straight to the worst, what I'm about to offer isn't really a short story at all but a sort of prose home movie, and those who have seen the footage have strongly advised me against nurturing any elaborate distribution plans for it. The dissenting group, it's my privilege and headache to divulge, consists of the three featured players themselves, two female, one male. We'll take the leading lady first, who, I believe, would prefer to be briefly described as a languid, sophisticated type. She feels that things might have gone along well enough if I'd just done something about a fifteen- or twenty-minute scene in which she blows her nose several times —snipped it out, I gather. She says it's disgusting to watch somebody keep blowing her nose. The other lady of the ensemble, a svelte twilight soubrette, objects to my having, so to speak, photographed her in her old housecoat. Neither of these two lovelies (as they've hinted they'd like to be called) takes any very shrill exception to my over-all exploitive purposes. For a terribly simple reason, really. If, to me, a somewhat reddening one. They know from experience that I burst into tears at the first harsh or remonstrative word. It's the leading man, however, who has made the most eloquent appeal to me to call off the production. *He* feels that the plot hinges on mysticism, or religious mystification—in any case, he makes it very clear, a too vividly apparent transcendent element of sorts, which he says he's worried can only expedite, move up, the day and hour of my professional undoing. People are already shaking their heads over me, and any immediate further professional use on my part of the word "God," except as a familiar, healthy American expletive, will be taken—or, rather, confirmed—as the very worst kind of name-dropping and a sure sign that I'm going straight to the dogs. Which is, of course, something to give any normal fainthearted man, and particularly writing man, pause. And it does. But only pause. For a point of objection, however eloquent, is only as good as it is applicable.

The fact is, I've been producing prose home movies, off and on, since I was fifteen. Somewhere in "The Great Gatsby" (which was my "Tom Sawyer" when I was twelve), the youthful narrator remarks that everybody suspects himself of having at least one of the cardinal virtues, and he goes on to say that he thinks his, bless his heart, is honesty. *Mine,* I think, is that I know the difference between a mystical story and a love story. I say that my current offering isn't a mystical story, or a religiously mystifying story, at all. *I* say it's a compound, or multiple, love story, pure and complicated.

The plot line itself, to finish up, is largely the result of a rather unholy collaborative effort. Almost all the facts to follow (slowly, *calmly* to follow) were originally given to me in hideously spaced installments, and in, to me, somewhat harrowingly private sittings, by the three player-characters themselves. Not one of the three, I might well add, showed any noticeably soaring talent for brevity of detail or compression of incident. A shortcoming, I'm afraid, that will be carried over to this, the final, or shooting, version. I can't excuse it, regrettably, but I insist on trying to explain it. We are, all four of us, blood relatives, and we speak a kind of esoteric, family language, a sort of semantic geometry in which the shortest distance between any two points is a fullish circle.

One last advisory word: Our family's surname is Glass. In just a moment, the youngest Glass

boy will be seen reading an exceedingly lengthy
letter (which will be reprinted here *in full,* I can
safely promise) sent to him by his eldest living
brother, Buddy Glass. The style of the letter,
I'm told, bears a considerably more than passing
resemblance to the style, or written mannerisms,
of this narrator, and the general reader will no
doubt jump to the heady conclusion that the
writer of the letter and I are one and the same
person. Jump he will, and, I'm afraid, jump he
should. We will, however, leave this Buddy
Glass in the third person from here on in. At
least, I see no good reason to take him out of it.

TEN-THIRTY on a Monday morning in November of 1955, Zooey Glass, a young man of
twenty-five, was seated in a very full bath, reading a four-year-old letter. It was an almost end-
less-looking letter, typewritten on several pages
of second-sheet yellow paper, and he was having
some little trouble keeping it propped up
against the two dry islands of his knees. At his
right, a dampish-looking cigarette was balanced
on the edge of the built-in enamel soapcatch,
and evidently it was burning well enough, for
every now and then he picked it off and took
a drag or two, without quite having to look up
from his letter. His ashes invariably fell into the
tub water, either straightway or down one of
the letter pages. He seemed unaware of the mes-
siness of the arrangement. He did seem aware,
though, if only just, that the heat of the water

was beginning to have a dehydrating effect on him. The longer he sat reading—or re-reading —the more often and the less absently he used the back of his wrist to blot his forehead and upper lip.

In Zooey, be assured early, we are dealing with the complex, the overlapping, the cloven, and at least two dossier-like paragraphs ought to be got in right here. To start with, he was a small young man, and extremely slight of body. From the rear—particularly where his vertebrae were visible—he might almost have passed for one of those needy metropolitan children who are sent out every summer to endowed camps to be fattened and sunned. Close up, either full-face or in profile, he was surpassingly handsome, even spectacularly so. His eldest sister (who modestly prefers to be identified here as a Tuckahoe homemaker) has asked me to describe him as looking like "the blue-eyed Jewish-Irish Mohican scout who died in your arms at the roulette table at Monte Carlo." A more general and surely less parochial view was that his face had been just barely saved from too-handsomeness, not to say gorgeousness, by virtue of one ear's protruding slightly more than the other. I myself hold a very different opinion from either of these. I submit that Zooey's face was close to being a wholly beautiful face. As such, it was of course vulnerable to the same variety of glibly undaunted and usually specious evaluations that any legitimate art object is. I think it just remains to be said that any one of a hundred every-day menaces—a car accident, a head cold, a lie before breakfast—could have disfigured or coarsened his bounteous good looks in a day or a second. But what was undiminishable, and, as already so flatly suggested, a joy of a kind forever, was an authentic *esprit* superimposed over his entire face—especially at the eyes, where it was often as arresting as a Harlequin mask, and, on occasion, much more confounding.

By profession, Zooey was an actor, a leading man, in television, and had been for a little more than three years. He was, in fact, as "sought after" (and, according to vague second-hand reports that reached his family, as highly paid) as a young leading man in television perhaps can be who isn't at the same time a Hollywood or Broadway star with a ready-made national reputation. But possibly either of these statements, without elaboration, can lead to an overly clearcut line of conjecture. As it happened, Zooey had made a formal and serious début as a public performer at the age of seven. He was the second youngest of what had originally been seven brothers and sisters*—five boys and two girls—

---

* The aesthetic evil of a footnote seems in order just here, I'm afraid. In all that follows, only the two youngest of the seven children will be directly seen or heard. The remaining five, however, the senior five, will be stalking in and out of the plot with considerable frequency, like so many Banquo's ghosts. The reader, then, may care to know at the outset that in 1955 the eldest of the Glass children, Seymour, had been dead almost seven years. He committed suicide while vacationing in Florida with his wife. If alive, he would have been

all of whom, at rather conveniently spaced in-
tervals during childhood, had been heard regularly on a network radio program, a children's
quiz show called "It's a Wise Child." An age
difference of almost eighteen years between the
eldest of the Glass children, Seymour, and the
youngest, Franny, had helped very considerably
to allow the family to reserve a kind of dynastic
seating arrangement at the "Wise Child" micro-
phones, which lasted just over sixteen years—
from 1927 well into 1943, a span of years con-
necting the Charleston and B-17 Eras. (All this
data, I think, is to some degree relevant.) For all
the gaps and years between their individual hey-
days on the program, it may be said (with few,
and no really important, reservations) that all
seven of the children had managed to answer
over the air a prodigious number of alternately
deadly-bookish and deadly-cute questions—sent
in by listeners—with a freshness, an aplomb,
that was considered unique in commercial radio.

thirty-eight in 1955. The second-eldest child, Buddy, was
what is known in campus-catalogue parlance as "writer-in-
residence" at a girls' junior college in upper New York State.
He lived alone, in a small, unwinterized, unelectrified house
about a quarter of a mile away from a rather popular ski-
run. The next-eldest of the children, Boo Boo, was married
and the mother of three children. In November, 1955, she
was travelling in Europe with her husband and all three of
their children. In order of age, the twins, Walt and Waker,
come after Boo Boo. Walt had been dead just over ten years.
He was killed in a freakish explosion while he was with the
Army of Occupation in Japan. Waker, his junior by some
twelve minutes, was a Roman Catholic priest, and in November, 1955, he was in Ecuador, attending a Jesuit conference
of some kind.

Public response to the children was often hot and never tepid. In general, listeners were divided into two, curiously restive camps: those who held that the Glasses were a bunch of insufferably "superior" little bastards that should have been drowned or gassed at birth, and those who held that they were bona-fide underage wits and savants, of an uncommon, if unenviable, order. At this writing (1957), there are former listeners to "It's a Wise Child" who remember, with basically astonishing accuracy, many of the individual performances of each of the seven children. In this same thinning but still oddly coterielike group, the consensus is that, of all the Glass children, the eldest boy, Seymour, back in the late twenties and early thirties, had been the "best" to hear, the most consistently "rewarding." After Seymour, Zooey, the youngest boy in the family, is generally placed second in order of preference, or appeal. And since we have a singularly workaday interest in Zooey here, it may be appended that, as an ex-panelist on "It's a Wise Child," he had one almanaclike distinction among (or over) his brothers and sisters. Off and on, during their broadcasting years, all seven of the children had been fair game for the kind of child psychologist or professional educator who takes a special interest in extra-precocious children. In this cause, or service, Zooey had been, of all the Glasses, hands down, the most voraciously examined, interviewed, and poked at. Very notably, with no exceptions that

I know of, his experiences in the apparently divergent fields of clinical, social, and newsstand psychology had been costly for him, as though the places where he was examined had been uniformly alive with either highly contagious traumas or just plain old-fashioned germs. For example, in 1942 (with the everlasting disapproval of his two eldest brothers, both of whom were in the Army at the time) he had been tested by one research group alone, in Boston, on five separate occasions. (He was twelve during most of the sessions, and it's possible that the train rides—ten of them—held some attraction for him, at least in the beginning.) The main purpose of the five tests, one gathered, was to isolate and study, if possible, the source of Zooey's precocious wit and fancy. At the end of the fifth test, the subject was sent home to New York with three or four aspirins in an engraved envelope for his sniffles, which turned out to be bronchial pneumonia. Some six weeks later, a long-distance call came through from Boston at eleven-thirty at night, with much dropping of small coins in an ordinary pay phone, and an unidentified voice—with no intention, presumably, of sounding pedantically waggish—informed Mr. and Mrs. Glass that their son Zooey, at twelve, had an English vocabulary on an exact par with Mary Baker Eddy's, if he could be urged to use it.

To resume: The long, typewritten, four-year-old letter that Zooey had checked into the bathtub with, on this Monday morning in November, 1955, had obviously been taken out of its envelope and unfolded and refolded on too many private occasions during the four years, so that now it not only had an over-all *unappetitlich* appearance but was actually torn in several places, mostly along the creases. The author of the letter, as stated earlier, was Zooey's eldest living brother, Buddy. The letter itself was virtually endless in length, overwritten, teaching, repetitious, opinionated, remonstrative, condescending, embarrassing—and filled, to a surfeit, with affection. In short, it was exactly the kind of letter that a recipient, whether he wants to or not, carries around for some time in his hip pocket. And that professional writers of a type love to reproduce verbatim:

3/18/51

DEAR ZOOEY,

I've just finished decoding a long letter that came from Mother this morning, all about you and General Eisenhower's smile and small boys in the *Daily News* who fall down elevator shafts and when am I going to have my phone in New York taken *out* and get one installed up here in the *country,* where I really *need* it. Surely the only woman in the world who can write a letter in invisible italics. Dear Bessie. I get five hundred words of copy from her like clockwork every three months on the subject of my poor old private phone and how *stup*id it is to pay

Good Money every month for something nobody's ever even around to *use* any more. Which
is really a big fat lie. When I'm in town, I invariably sit talking by the hour with my old
friend Yama, the God of Death, and a private
phone's a must for our little chats. Anyway,
please tell her I haven't changed my mind. I
love that old phone with a passion. It was the
only really private property Seymour and I ever
had in Bessie's entire kibbutz. It's also essential
to my inner harmony to see Seymour's listing in
the goddam phone book every year. I like to
browse through the G's confidently. Be a good
boy and pass that message along for me. Not
quite word for word, but nicely. Be kinder to
Bessie, Zooey, when you can. I don't think I
mean because she's our mother, but because she's
weary. You will after you're thirty or so, when
everybody slows down a little (even you, maybe),
but try harder now. It isn't enough to treat her
with the doting brutality of an apache dancer
toward his partner—which she understands, incidentally, whether you think so or not. You forget that she thrives on sentimentality almost as
much as Les does.

My telephone problems aside, Bessie's current
letter is really a Zooey letter. I'm to write and
tell you that you have your Whole Life Before
You and that it's Criminal if you don't go after
your Ph.D. before you go in for the actor's life
in a big way. She doesn't say what she'd like
you to get the Ph.D. in, but I assume Math

rather than Greek, you dirty little bookworm. At any rate, I gather that she wants you to have something to Fall Back On if for some reason the acting career doesn't work out. Which may be very sound, and probably is, but I don't feel like coming right out and saying so. It happens to be one of those days when I see everybody in the family, including myself, through the wrong end of a telescope. I actually had to struggle at the mailbox this morning to know who Bessie was when I saw her name on the return address of the envelope. For one good enough reason, Advanced Writing 24-A loaded me up with thirty-eight short stories to drag tearfully home for the weekend. Thirty-seven of them will be about a shy, reclusive Pennsylvania Dutch lesbian who Wants To Write, told first-person by a lecherous hired hand. In dialect.

I take it for granted you *know* that for all the years I've been moving my literary whore's cubicle from college to college, I still don't have even a B.A. It seems a century ago, but I think there were two reasons, originally, why I didn't take a degree. (Just kindly sit still. This is the first time I've written to you in years.) One, I was a proper snob in college, as only an old Wise Child alumnus and future lifetime English-major can be, and I didn't want any degrees if all the ill-read literates and radio announcers and pedagogical dummies I knew had them by the peck. And, two, Seymour had his Ph.D. at an age when most young Americans are just getting out of high school, and since it was too late for me to catch up with him in style, I wasn't having any. Of course, too, I knew for certain when I was your age that I'd never be forced to teach, that if my Muses failed to provide for me, I'd go grind lenses somewhere, like Booker T. Washington. In any particular sense, though, I don't think I have any academic regrets. On especially black days I sometimes tell myself that if I'd loaded up with degrees when I was able, I might not now be teaching anything quite so collegiate and hopeless as Advanced Writing 24-A. But that's probably bunk. The cards are stacked (quite properly, I imagine) against all professional aesthetes, and no doubt we all deserve the dark, wordy, academic deaths we all sooner or later die.

I do think your case is a lot different from mine. Anyway, I don't think I'm really on Bessie's side. If it's Security you want, or that Bessie wants for you, your M.A. will at least always qualify you to pass out logarithm tables at any dreary boys' prep school in the country, and most colleges. On the other hand, your beautiful Greek will do you almost no good at all on any good-size campus unless you have a Ph.D., living as we do in a brass-hat, brass-mortarboard world. (Of course, you can always move to Athens. Sunny *old* Athens.) But the more I think of it, the more I think to hell with more degrees for you. The fact is, if you want to know, I can't help thinking you'd make a damn site better-

adjusted actor if Seymour and I hadn't thrown
in the Upanishads and the Diamond Sutra and
Eckhart and all our other old loves with the rest
of your recommended home reading when you
were small. By rights, an actor should travel
fairly light. When we were kids, S. and I once
had a beautiful lunch with John Barrymore. He
was bright as hell, and full of lore, but he wasn't
burdened down with any of the cumbersome
luggage of a too formal education. I mention
this because I was talking to a rather pompous
Orientalist over the weekend, and at one point,
during a very deep, metaphysical lull in the conversation, I told him I had a little brother who
once got over an unhappy love affair by trying
to translate the Mundaka Upanishad into classi-
cal Greek. (He laughed uproariously—you know
the way Orientalists laugh.)

I wish to God I had some idea what will happen to you as an actor. You're a born one, certainly. Even our Bessie knows that. And surely
you and Franny are the only beauties in the
family. But where will you act? Have you
thought about it? The movies? If so, I'm scared
stiff that if ever you gain any weight you'll be
as victimized as the next young actor into con-
tributing to the reliable Hollywood amalgam of
prizefighter and mystic, gunman and underprivi-
leged child, cowhand and Man's Conscience,
and the rest. Will you be content with that
standard box-office schmalz? Or will you dream
of something a little more cosmic—zum Beispiel,

playing Pierre or Andrey in a Technicolor production of War and Peace, with stunning battlefield scenes, and all the nuances of characterization left out (on the ground that they're novelistic and unphotogenic), and Anna Magnani daringly cast as Natasha (just to keep the production classy and Honest), and gorgeous incidental music by Dmitri Popkin, and all the male leads intermittently rippling their jaw muscles to show they're under great emotional stress, and a World Première at the Winter Garden, under floodlights, with Molotov and Milton Berle and Governor Dewey introducing the celebrities as they come into the theatre. (By celebrities I mean, of course, old Tolstoy-lovers —Senator Dirksen, Zsa Zsa Gabor, Gayelord Hauser, Georgie Jessel, Charles of the Ritz.) How does that sound? And if you go into the theatre, will you have any illusions about *that?* Have you ever seen a really beautiful production of, say, The Cherry Orchard? Don't say you have. Nobody has. You may have seen "inspired" productions, "competent" productions, but never anything beautiful. Never one where Chekhov's talent is matched, nuance for nuance, idiosyncrasy for idiosyncrasy, by every soul onstage. You worry *hell* out of me, Zooey. Forgive the pessimism, if not the sonority. But I know how much you demand from a thing, you little bastard. And I've had the hellish experience of sitting next to you at the theatre. I can so clearly see you demanding something from the performing arts that just isn't residual there. For heaven's sake, be careful.

Granted I'm off today. I keep a good neurotic's calendar, and it's three years, to the day, since Seymour killed himself. Did I ever tell you what happened when I went down to Florida to bring back the body? I wept like a slob on the plane for five solid hours. Carefully adjusting my veil from time to time so that no one across the aisle could see me—I had a seat to myself, thank God. About five minutes before the plane landed, I became aware of people talking in the seat behind me. A woman was saying, with all of Back Bay Boston and most of Harvard Square in her voice, ". . . and the *next morning,* mind you, they took a pint of pus out of that lovely young body of hers." That's all I remember hearing, but when I got off the plane a few minutes later and the Bereaved Widow came toward me all in Bergdorf Goodman black, I had the Wrong Expression on my face. I was grinning. Which is exactly the way I feel today, for no really good reason. Against my better judgment, I feel certain that somewhere very near here—the first house down the road, maybe—there's a good poet dying, but also somewhere very near here somebody's having a hilarious pint of pus taken from her lovely young body, and I can't be running back and forth forever between grief and high delight.

Last month, Dean Sheeter (whose name usually transports Franny when I mention it) approached me with his gracious smile and bull whip, and I am now lecturing to the faculty, their wives, and a few oppressively deep-type undergraduates every Friday on Zen and Mahayana Buddhism. A feat, I haven't a doubt, that will eventually win me the Eastern Philosophy Chair in Hell. The point is, I'm now on the campus five days a week instead of four, and what with my own work at nights and on weekends, I have almost no time to do any elective thinking. Which is my plaintive way of saying that I do worry about you and Franny when I get a chance, but not nearly so often as I'd like to. What I'm really trying to tell you is that Bessie's letter had very little to do with my sitting down in a sea of ashtrays to write to you today. She shoots me some priority information about you and Franny every week and I never do anything about it, so it isn't that. What brings this on is something that happened to me at the local supermarket today. (No new paragraph. I'll spare you that.) I was standing at the meat counter, waiting for some rib lamb chops to be cut. A young mother and her little girl were waiting around, too. The little girl was about four, and, to pass the time, she leaned her back against the glass showcase and stared up at my unshaven face. I told her she was about the prettiest little girl I'd seen all day. Which made sense to her; she nodded. I said I'd bet she had a lot of boy friends. I got the same nod again. I asked her how many boy friends she had. She held up two fingers. "Two!" I said. "That's a lot of boy friends. What are their names, sweetheart?" Said she, in a piercing voice, *"Bobby and Dorothy."* I grabbed my lamb chops and ran. But that's exactly what brought on this letter—much more than Bessie's insistence that I write to you about Ph.D.s and acting. That, and a haiku-style poem I found in the hotel room where Seymour shot himself. It was written in pencil on the desk blotter: "The little girl on the plane/ Who turned her doll's head around/ To look at me." With these two things on my mind, I thought as I was driving home from the supermarket that at long last I could write to you and tell you *why* S. and I took over your and Franny's education as early and as highhandedly as we did. We've never put it into words for you, and I think it's high time one of us did. But now I'm not so sure I can do it. The little girl at the meat counter is gone, and I can't quite see the polite face of the little doll on the plane. And the old horror of being a professional writer, and the usual stench of words that goes with it, is beginning to drive me out of my seat. It seems terribly important to try, though.

The age differences in the family always seemed to add unnecessarily and perversely to our problems. Not really between S. and the twins and Boo Boo and me, but between the two twosomes of you and Franny and S. and me. Seymour and I were both adults—he was even

long out of college—by the time you and
Franny were both able to read. At that stage,
we had no real urge even to push our favorite
classics at the two of you—not, anyway, with the
same gusto that we had at the twins or Boo Boo.
We knew there's no keeping a born scholar
ignorant, and at heart, I think, we didn't really
want to, but we were nervous, even frightened,
at the statistics on child pedants and academic
weisenheimers who grow up into faculty-recrea-
tion-room savants. Much, much more important,
though, Seymour had already begun to believe
(and I agreed with him, as far as I was able to
see the point) that education by any name would
smell as sweet, and maybe much sweeter, if it
didn't begin with a quest for knowledge at all
but with a quest, as Zen would put it, for no-
knowledge. Dr. Suzuki says somewhere that to
be in a state of pure consciousness—*satori*—is
to be with God before he said, Let there be
light. Seymour and I thought it might be a good
thing to hold back this light from you and
Franny (at least as far as we were able), and all
the many lower, more fashionable lighting effects—the arts, sciences, classics, languages—till
you were both able at least to conceive of a state
of being where the mind knows the source of all
light. We thought it would be wonderfully constructive to at least (that is, if our own "limita-
tions" got in the way) tell you as much as we
knew about the men—the saints, the arhats, the
bodhisattvas, the jivanmuktas—who knew some-

thing or everything about this state of being. That is, we wanted you both to know who and what Jesus and Gautama and Lao-tse and Shankaracharya and Hui-neng and Sri Ramakrishna, etc., were before you knew too much or anything about Homer or Shakespeare or even Blake or Whitman, let alone George Washington and his cherry tree or the definition of a peninsula or how to parse a sentence. That, anyway, was the big idea. Along with all this, I suppose I'm trying to say that I know how bitterly you resent the years when S. and I were regularly conducting home seminars, and the metaphysical sittings in particular. I just hope that one day—preferably when we're both blind drunk—we can talk about it. (Meantime, I can only say that neither Seymour nor I ever had a notion, that far back, that you were going to grow up into an actor. We *should* have, no doubt, but we didn't. If we had, I feel certain S. would have tried to do something constructive about it. Surely somewhere there must be a special prep course for Nirvana and points East designed strictly for actors, and I think S. would have found it.) The paragraph should close, but I can't stop muttering. You'll wince at what comes next, but come it must. I think you know that I had the best intentions of checking in now and then after S.'s death to see how you and Franny were holding up. You were eighteen, and I didn't worry about you overly. Although I did hear from a gossipy little snip in

one of my classes that you had a reputation in
your college dorm for going off and sitting in
meditation for ten hours at a time, and *that*
made me think. But Franny was *thirteen* at the
time. I simply couldn't move, though. I was
afraid to come home. I wasn't afraid you'd both,
in tears, take up a position across the room and
fire the complete set of Max Mueller's Sacred
Books of the East at me, one by one. (Which
would have been masochistic ecstasy for me,
probably.) But I *was* afraid of the questions
(much more than the accusations) you might
both put to me. As I remember very well, I let
a whole year go by after the funeral before I
came back to New York at all. After that, it was
easy enough to come in for birthdays and holi-
days and be reasonably sure that questions
would run to when my next book would be
finished and had I done any skiing lately, etc.
You've even both been up here on many a
weekend in the last couple of years, and though
we've talked and talked and talked, we've all
agreed not to say a word. Today is the first time
I've really wanted to speak up. The deeper I
get into this goddam letter, the more I lose the
courage of my convictions. But I swear to you
that I had a perfectly communicable little vision
of truth (lamb-chop division) this afternoon the
very instant that child told me her boy friends'
names were Bobby and Dorothy. Seymour once
said to me—in a crosstown bus, of all places—
that all legitimate religious study *must* lead to

unlearning the differences, the illusory differences, between boys and girls, animals and
stones, day and night, heat and cold. That suddenly hit me at the meat counter, and it seemed
a matter of life and death to drive home at
seventy miles an hour to get a letter off to you.
Oh, God, how I wish I'd grabbed a pencil right
there in the supermarket and not trusted the
roads home. Maybe it's just as well, though.
There are times when I think you've forgiven
S. more completely than any of us have. Waker
once said something very interesting to me on
that subject—in fact, I'm merely parroting what
he said to me. He said you were the only one
who was bitter about S.'s suicide and the only
one who really forgave him for it. The rest of
us, he said, were outwardly unbitter and in-
wardly unforgiving. That may be truer than
true. How can I know? All I do know for certain is that I had something happy and exciting
to tell you—and on just one side of the paper,
doublespaced—and I knew when I got home
that it was mostly gone, or all gone, and there
was nothing left to do but go through the mo-
tions. Lecture you on Ph.D.s and the actor's life.
How messy, how funny, and how Seymour himself would have smiled and smiled—and probably assured me, and all of us, not to worry
about it.

Enough. *Act,* Zachary Martin Glass, when and
where you want to, since you feel you must, but
do it *with all your might*. If you do anything at

all beautiful on a stage, anything nameless and joy-making, anything above and beyond the call of theatrical ingenuity, S. and I will both rent tuxedos and rhinestone hats and solemnly come around to the stage door with bouquets of snap-dragons. In any case, for what little it's worth, please count on my affection and support, at whatever distance.

BUDDY

As always, my passes at omniscience are ab-surd, but you, of all people, should be polite to the part of me that comes out merely clever. Years ago, in my earliest and pastiest days as a would-be writer, I once read a new story aloud to S. and Boo Boo. When I was finished, Boo Boo said flatly (but looking over at Seymour) that the story was "too clever." S. shook his head, beaming away at me, and said cleverness was my permanent affliction, my wooden leg, and that it was in the worst possible taste to draw the group's attention to it. As one limping man to another, old Zooey, let's be courteous and kind to each other.

Much love,
B.

THE last, the under, page of the four-year-old letter was stained a sort of off-cordovan color, and it was torn in two places along the folds. Zooey, finished reading, treated it with some lit-tle care as he put the letter back into page-one order. He tapped the pages, to even them out,

against his dry knees. He frowned. Then, mer-
curially, as though he'd read the letter, by God,
for the last time in his life, he stuffed it like so
much excelsior into its envelope. He placed the
thick envelope on the side of the tub and began
to play a little game with it. With one finger he
tapped the loaded envelope back and forth
along the tub edge, seeing, apparently, if he
could keep it in motion without letting it fall
into the tub water. After a good five minutes of
this, he gave the envelope a faulty tap and had
to reach out quickly and grab it. Which ended
the game. Keeping the retrieved envelope in his
hand, he sat lower, deeper, in the water, letting
his knees submerge. He stared abstractedly for a
minute or two at the tiled wall beyond the foot
of the tub, then glanced at his cigarette on the
soapcatch, picked it off, and took a couple of test
drags on it, but it had gone out. He sat up
again, very abruptly, with a great slosh of tub
water, and dropped his dry left hand over the
side of the tub. A typewritten manuscript was
lying, face up, on the bathmat. He picked it up
and brought it aboard, as it were. He stared at
it briefly, then inserted his four-year-old letter
in the middle pages, where the stapling in a
manuscript is tightest. He then propped the
manuscript against his now wet knees, an inch
or so above the waterline, and began to turn the
pages. When he came to page 9, he folded the
manuscript, magazine-style, and began to read
or to study.

The role of "Rick" had been heavily under-
lined with a soft-lead pencil.

TINA (*morosely*): Oh, darling, darling, darling.
I'm not much good to you, am I?

RICK: Don't say that. Don't ever say that, you
hear me?

TINA: It's true, though. I'm a jinx. I'm a horrible jinx. If it hadn't been for me, Scott Kincaid
would have assigned you to the Buenos Aires office
ages ago. I spoiled all that. (*Goes over to window*)
I'm one of the little foxes that spoil the grapes. I
feel like someone in a terribly sophisticated play.
The funny part is, I'm not sophisticated. I'm not
anything. I'm just me. (*Turns*) Oh, Rick, Rick, I'm
scared. What's happened to us? I can't seem to find
us anymore. I reach out and reach out and we're
just not there. I'm frightened. I'm a frightened
child. (*Looks out window*) I hate this rain. Sometimes I see me dead in it.

RICK (*quietly*): My darling, isn't that a line from
"A Farewell to Arms"?

TINA (*Turns, furious*): Get out of here. Get out!
Get out of here before I jump out of this window.
Do you hear me?

RICK (*grabbing her*): Now you listen to me. You
beautiful little moron. You adorable, childish, self-
dramatizing—

Zooey's reading was suddenly interrupted by
his mother's voice—importunate, quasi-construc-
tive—addressing him from outside the bathroom
door: "Zooey? Are you still in the tub?"

"*Yes,* I'm still in the tub. Why?"

"I want to come in for just a teeny minute.
I have something for you."

"I'm in the tub, for God's sake, Mother."

"I'll just be a *min*ute, for goodness' sake. Pull the shower curtain."

Zooey took a parting look at the page he had been reading, then closed the manuscript and dropped it over the side of the tub. "Jesus Christ almighty," he said. "Sometimes I see me dead in the rain." A nylon shower curtain, scarlet, with a design of canary-yellow sharps, flats, and clefs on it, was bunched up at the foot of the tub, attached with plastic rings to an overhead chromium bar. Sitting forward, Zooey reached for it and shot it the length of the tub, closing himself off from view. "All right. *God.* Come in if you're coming in," he said. His voice had no conspicuous actor's mannerisms, but it was rather excessively vibrant; it "carried" implacably when he had no interest in controlling it. Years earlier, as a child panelist on "It's a Wise Child," he had been advised repeatedly to keep his distance from the microphone.

The door opened, and Mrs. Glass, a medium-stout woman in a hairnet, sidled into the bathroom. Her age, under any circumstance, was fiercely indeterminate, but never more so than when she was wearing a hairnet. Her entrances into rooms were usually verbal as well as physical. "I don't know how you can stay in the tub the way you do." She closed the door behind her instantly, as someone does who has been waging a long, long war on behalf of her progeny against post-bath drafts. "It isn't even healthy," she said.

"Do you know how long you've been in that tub? Exactly forty-five—"

"Don't tell me! Just don't tell me, Bessie."

"What do you mean, don't *tell* you?"

"Just what I said. Leave me the goddam illusion you haven't been out there counting the minutes I've—"

"Nobody's been counting any *mi*nutes, young man," Mrs. Glass said. She was already very busy. She had brought into the bathroom a small, oblong package wrapped in white paper and tied with gold tinsel. It appeared to contain an object roughly the size of the Hope diamond or an irrigation attachment. Mrs. Glass narrowed her eyes at it and picked at the tinsel with her fingers. When the knot didn't give, she applied her teeth to it.

She was wearing her usual at-home vesture—what her son Buddy (who was a writer, and consequently, as Kafka, no less, has told us, *not a nice man*) called her pre-notification-of-death uniform. It consisted mostly of a hoary midnight-blue Japanese kimono. She almost invariably wore it throughout the apartment during the day. With its many occultish-looking folds, it also served as the repository for the paraphernalia of a very heavy cigarette smoker and an amateur handyman; two oversized pockets had been added at the hips, and they usually contained two or three packs of cigarettes, several match folders, a screwdriver, a claw-end hammer, a Boy Scout knife that had once belonged

to one of her sons, and an enamel faucet handle
or two, plus an assortment of screws, nails, hinges,
and ball-bearing casters—all of which tended to
make Mrs. Glass chink faintly as she moved
about in her large apartment. For ten years or
more, both of her daughters had often, if impo-
tently, conspired to throw out this veteran kimono. (Her married daughter, Boo Boo, had
intimated that it might have to be given a coup
de grâce with a blunt instrument before it was
laid away in a wastebasket.) However Oriental
the wrapper had originally been designed to
look, it didn't detract an iota from the single,
impactful impression that Mrs. Glass, *chez elle,*
made on a certain type of observer. The Glasses
lived in an old but, categorically, not unfashion-
able apartment house in the East Seventies,
where possibly two-thirds of the more mature
women tenants owned fur coats and, on leaving
the building on a bright weekday morning,
might at least conceivably be found, a half hour
or so later, getting in or out of one of the eleva-
tors at Lord & Taylor's or Saks or Bonwit Tel-
ler's. In this distinctly Manhattanesque locale,
Mrs. Glass was (from an undeniably hoyden
point of view) a rather refreshing eyesore. She
looked, first, as if she never, never left the building at all, but that *if* she did, she would be wearing a dark shawl and she would be going in the
general direction of O'Connell Street, there to
claim the body of one of her half-Irish, half-
Jewish sons, who, through some clerical error,

had just been shot dead by the Black and Tans.

Zooey's voice suddenly and suspiciously spoke up: "*Mother?* What in Christ's name are you doing out there?"

Mrs. Glass had undressed the package and now stood reading the fine print on the back of a carton of toothpaste. "Just kindly button that lip of yours," she said, rather absently. She went over to the medicine cabinet. It was stationed above the washbowl, against the wall. She opened its mirror-faced door and surveyed the congested shelves with the eye—or, rather, the masterly squint—of a dedicated medicine-cabinet gardener. Before her, in overly luxuriant rows, was a host, so to speak, of golden pharmaceuticals, plus a few technically less indigenous whatnots. The shelves bore iodine, Mercurochrome, vitamin capsules, dental floss, aspirin, Anacin, Bufferin, Argyrol, Musterole, Ex-Lax, Milk of Magnesia, Sal Hepatica, Aspergum, two Gillette razors, one Schick Injector razor, two tubes of shaving cream, a bent and somewhat torn snapshot of a fat black-and-white cat asleep on a porch railing, three combs, two hairbrushes, a bottle of Wildroot hair ointment, a bottle of Fitch Dandruff Remover, a small, unlabelled box of glycerine suppositories, Vicks Nose Drops, Vicks VapoRub, six bars of castile soap, the stubs of three tickets to a 1946 musical comedy ("Call Me Mister"), a tube of depilatory cream, a box of Kleenex, two seashells, an assortment of used-looking emery boards, two jars of cleansing cream, three pairs of scissors, a nail file, an un-clouded blue marble (known to marble shooters, at least in the twenties, as a "purey"), a cream for contracting enlarged pores, a pair of tweez-ers, the strapless chassis of a girl's or woman's gold wristwatch, a box of bicarbonate of soda, a girl's boarding-school class ring with a chipped onyx stone, a bottle of Stopette—and, inconceiv-ably or no, quite a good deal more. Mrs. Glass briskly reached up and took down an object from the bottom shelf and dropped it, with a muffled, tinny bang, into the wastebasket. "I'm putting some of that new toothpaste they're all raving about in here for you," she announced, without turning around, and made good her word. "I want you to stop using that crazy pow-der. It's going to take *all* the lovely enamel off your teeth. You *have* lovely teeth. The least you can do is take proper—"

"Who said so?" A sound of agitated tub water came from behind the shower curtain. "Who the hell said it's going to take all the lovely enamel off my teeth?"

"*I* did." Mrs. Glass gave her garden a final critical glance. "Just please use it." She nudged an unopened box of Sal Hepatica a little with the trowel of her extended fingers to align it with the other sempervirents in its row, and then closed the cabinet door. She turned on the cold-water tap. "I'd like to know who washes their hands and then doesn't clean the bowl up after them," she said grimly. "This is supposed to be

a family of all adults." She increased the pressure of the water and cleansed the bowl briefly
but thoroughly with one hand. "I don't suppose
you've spoken to your little sister yet," she said,
and turned to look at the shower curtain.

"No, I have not spoken to my little sister yet.
How 'bout getting the hell out of here now?"

"Why haven't you?" Mrs. Glass demanded. "I
don't think that's nice, Zooey. I don't think
that's nice at *all*. I asked you particularly to
please go see if there's anything—"

"In the first place, Bessie, I just got up about
an hour ago. In the second place, I talked to her
for two solid hours last night, and I don't think
she frankly wants to talk to any goddam one of
us today. And in the third place, if you don't get
out of this bathroom I'm going to set fire to this
ugly goddam curtain. I mean it, Bessie."

Somewhere in the middle of these three illus-
trative points, Mrs. Glass had left off listening
and sat down. "Sometimes I could almost murder Buddy for not having a phone," she said.
"It's so un*nece*ssary. How can a grown man *live*
like that—no *phone*, no *any*thing? No one has
any desire to invade his *privacy*, if that's what he
wants, but I certainly don't think it's necessary
to live like a *herm*it." She stirred irritably, and
crossed her legs. "It isn't even safe, for heaven's
sake! Suppose he broke his leg or something like
that. Way off in the *woods* like that. I worry
about it all the time."

"You do, eh? Which do you worry about? His

breaking a leg or his not having a phone when you want him to?"

"I worry about *both,* young man, for your information."

"Well . . . don't. Don't waste your time. You're so stupid, Bessie. Why are you so stupid? You know Buddy, for God's sake. If he were twenty *miles* in the woods, with both legs broken and a goddam *arrow* sticking out of his back, he'd crawl back to his cave just to make certain nobody sneaked in to try on his galoshes while he was out." A short, pleasurable, if somewhat ghoulish, guffaw sounded behind the curtain. "Take my word for it. He cares too much about his goddam privacy to die in any woods."

"Nobody said anything about *dy*ing," Mrs. Glass said. She gave her hairnet a minor and needless adjustment. "I've been trying the *whole entire* morning to get those people that live down the road from him on the phone. They don't even answer. It's in*fur*iating not to be able to get him. How many times I've *begged* him to take that crazy phone out of his and Seymour's old room. It isn't even *nor*mal. When something really comes *up* and he *needs* one— It's infuriating. I tried twice last night, and about four times this—"

"What's all this 'infuriating' business? In the first place, why should some strangers down the road be at our beck and call?"

"Nobody's talking about anybody being at our beck and *call,* Zooey. Just don't be so fresh, please. For your information, I'm *very* worried about that child. *And* I think Buddy should be told about this whole thing. Just for your infor-*ma*tion, I don't think he'd ever forgive me if I didn't get in touch with him at a time like this."

"All right, then! Why don't you call the col-lege, instead of bothering his neighbors? He wouldn't be in his cave anyway at this time of day—you know that."

"Just kindly lower that voice of yours, please, young man. Nobody's deaf. For your informa-tion, I have called the college. I've learned from experience that that does absolutely no good whatsoever. They just leave messages on his desk, and I don't think he ever goes anywhere *near* his office anyway." Mrs. Glass abruptly leaned her weight forward, without getting up, and reached out and picked up something from the top of the laundry hamper. "Do you have a washrag back there?" she asked.

"The word is 'washcloth,' not 'washrag,' and all I want, God damn it, Bessie, is to be left alone in this bathroom. That's my one simple desire. If I'd wanted this place to fill up with every fat Irish rose that passes by, I'd've said so. Now, c'mon. Get out."

"Zooey," Mrs. Glass said patiently. "I'm hold-ing a clean washrag in my *hand*. Do you or don't you want it? Just yes or no, please."

"Oh, my God! Yes. Yes. *Yes*. More than any-thing in the world. Throw it over."

"I won't *throw* it over, I'll hand it to you. Al-

ways throw everything, in this family." Mrs.
Glass got up, took three steps over to the shower
curtain, and waited for a disembodied hand to
claim the washcloth.

"Thanks a million. Clear out of here now,
please. I've lost about ten pounds already."

"It's no *won*der! You sit there in that tub till
you're practically blue in the face, and then you
—What's *this?*" With immense interest, Mrs.
Glass bent down and picked up the manuscript
Zooey had been reading before she made her entrance into the room. "Is this the new script Mr.
LeSage sent over?" she asked. "On the *floor?*"
She didn't get an answer. It was as if Eve had
asked Cain whether that wasn't his lovely new
hoe lying out there in the rain. "That's a marvellous place to put a *man*uscript, I must say."
She transported the manuscript over to the window and placed it with care on the radiator. She
looked down at it, appearing to inspect it for
wetness. The window blind had been lowered—
Zooey had done all his bathtub reading by the
light from the three-bulb overhead fixture—but
a fraction of morning light inched under the
blind and onto the title page of the manuscript.
Mrs. Glass tilted her head to one side, the better to read the title, at the same time taking a
pack of king-size cigarettes from her kimono
pocket. " 'The Heart Is an Autumn Wanderer,' "
she read, mused, aloud. "Unusual title."

The response from behind the shower curtain was a trifle delayed but delighted. "It's a what? It's a what kind of title?"

Mrs. Glass's guard was already up. She backed up and re-seated herself, a lighted cigarette in her hand. "Un*us*ual, I said. I didn't say it was *beau*tiful or anything, so just—"

"Ahh, by George. You have to get up pretty early in the morning to get anything really classy past you, Bessie girl. You know what your heart is, Bessie? Would you like to know what your heart is? *Your heart,* Bessie, is an autumn garage. How's that for a catchy title, eh? By God, many people—many *uninformed* people—think Seymour and Buddy are the only goddam men of letters in this family. When I *think,* when I sit down for a minute and think of the sensitive prose, and garages, I throw away every day of my—"

"All right, all right, young man," Mrs. Glass said. Whatever her taste in television-play titles, or her aesthetics in general, a flicker came into her eyes—no more than a flicker, but a flicker— of connoisseurlike, if perverse, relish for her youngest, and only handsome, son's style of bullying. For a split second, it displaced the look of all-round wear and, plainly, specific worry that had been on her face since she entered the bathroom. However, she was almost immediately back on the defensive: "What's the matter with that title? It *is* very unusual. You! You don't think anything's unusual or beautiful! I've never once heard you—"

"*What? Who* doesn't? Exactly what don't I think isn't beautiful?" A minor groundswell sounded behind the shower curtain, as though a rather delinquent porpoise were suddenly at play. "Listen, I don't care what you say about my race, creed, or religion, Fatty, but don't tell me I'm not sensitive to beauty. That's my Achilles' heel, and don't you forget it. To me, *ev*erything is beautiful. Show me a pink sunset and I'm limp, by God. *Any*thing. 'Peter Pan.' Even before the curtain goes up at 'Peter Pan,' I'm a goddam puddle of tears. And you have the gall to try to tell me I'm—"

"Oh, shut up," Mrs. Glass said, absently. She gave a great sigh. Then, with a tense expression, she dragged deeply on her cigarette and, exhaling the smoke through her nostrils, said— or, rather, erupted—"Oh, I *wish* I knew what I'm supposed to do with that child!" She took a deep breath. "I'm absolutely at the end of my *rope*." She gave the shower curtain an X-ray-like look. "You're none of you any help whatsoever. But none! Your *father* doesn't even like to *talk* about anything like this. You know that! He's worried, too, naturally—I know that look on his face—but he simply will not face anything." Mrs. Glass's mouth tightened. "He's never faced anything as long as I've known him. He thinks anything pe*cul*iar or un*pleas*ant will just go away if he turns on the radio and some little schnook starts *sing*ing."

A great single roar of laughter came from

the closed-off Zooey. It was scarcely distinguishable from his guffaw, but there *was* a difference.

"Well, he does!" Mrs. Glass insisted, humorlessly. She sat forward. "Would you like to know what I honestly think?" she demanded. "*Would* you?"

"Bessie. For God's sake. You're going to tell me anyway, so what's the difference if I—"

"I honestly think—I *mean* this, now—I *honestly* think he keeps hoping to hear all you children on the radio again. I'm serious, now." Mrs. Glass took another deep breath. "Every single time your father turns on the radio, I honestly think he expects to tune in on 'It's a Wise Child' and hear all you children, *one by one,* answering questions again." She compressed her lips and paused, unconsciously, for additional emphasis. "And I mean all of you," she said, and abruptly straightened her posture a trifle. "That includes Seymour and Walt." She took a brisk but voluminous drag on her cigarette. "He lives entirely in the past. But entirely. He hardly ever even *watches* television, unless *you're* on. And don't laugh, Zooey. It isn't funny."

"Who in God's name is laughing?"

"Well, it's true! He has absolutely no conception of anything being really wrong with Franny. But none! Right after the eleven-o'clock news last night, what do you think he asks me? If I think Franny might like a tange*rine!* The child's laying there by the hour crying her eyes out if you say boo to her, and mumbling heaven knows *what* to herself, and your father wonders if maybe she'd like a tangerine. I could've killed him. The next time he—" Mrs. Glass broke off. She glared at the shower curtain. "What's so funny?" she demanded.

"Nothing. Nothing, nothing, nothing. I like the tangerine. All right, who else is being no help to you? Me. Les. Buddy. Who else? Pour your heart out to me, Bessie. Don't be reticent. That's the whole trouble with this family—we keep things bottled up too much."

"Oh, you're about as funny as a crutch, young man," Mrs. Glass said. She took time to push a stray wisp of hair under the elastic of her hair-net. "Oh, I *wish* I could get Buddy on that crazy phone for a few minutes. The one person that's supposed to *know* about all this funny business." She reflected, with apparent rancor. "It never rains but it pours." She tapped her cigarette ash into her cupped left hand. "Boo Boo won't be back till the *tenth*. Waker I'd be *afraid* to tell about it, even if I knew how to get *hold* of him. I never saw a family like this in my entire life. I mean it. You're all supposed to be so in*tell*igent and everything, all you children, and not one of you is any help when the chips are down. Not one of you. I'm just a little bit sick of—"

"*What* chips, for God's sake? When what chips are down? What would you like us to do, Bessie? Go in there and live Franny's life for her?"

"Now, just stop that! Nobody's talking about anybody living her *life* for her. I'd simply like *some*body to go in that living room and find out what's what, *that's* what I'd like. I'd like to know just when that child intends to go back to college and finish her *year*. I'd like to know just when she intends to put something halfway *nour*ishing into her stomach. She's eaten practically nothing since she got home Saturday night —but nothing! I tried—not a half hour ago—to get her to take a nice cup of chicken broth. She took exactly two mouthfuls, and that's *all*. She threw *up* everything I got her to eat yesterday, practically." Mrs. Glass's voice stopped only long enough to reload, as it were. "She said maybe she'd eat a cheeseburger later on. Just what is this *cheese*burger business? From what I gather, she's practically been living on cheeseburgers and Cokes all semester so far. Is that what they feed a young girl at college these days? I know *one* thing. I'm certainly not going to feed a young girl that's as run-down as that child is on food that isn't even—"

"That's the spirit! Make it chicken broth or nothing. That's putting the ole foot down. If she's determined to have a nervous breakdown, the least we can do is see that she doesn't have it in peace."

"Just don't you be so *fresh,* young man—Oh, that mouth of yours! For your infor*ma*tion, I don't think it's at all impossible that the kind of food that child takes into her system hasn't a lot to do with this whole entire funny business. Even as a *child* you practically had to force that child to even touch her vegetables or any of the things that were *good* for her. You can't go on abusing the body indefinitely, year in, year out —regardless of what you think."

"You're absolutely right. You're absolutely right. It's staggering how you jump straight the hell into the heart of a matter. I'm goosebumps all over . . . By God, you inspire me. You inflame me, Bessie. You know what you've done? Do you realize what you've done? You've given this whole goddam issue a fresh, new, *Biblical* slant. I wrote four papers in college on the Crucifixion —five, really—and every one of them worried me half crazy because I thought something was missing. Now I know what it was. Now it's clear to me. I see Christ in an *entirely different light.* His unhealthy fanaticism. His rudeness to those nice, sane, conservative, tax-paying Pharisees. Oh, this is exciting! In your simple, straightforward, bigoted way, Bessie, you've sounded the missing keynote of the whole New Testament. *Improper diet.* Christ lived on cheeseburgers and Cokes. For all we know, he probably fed the mult—"

"Just stop that, now," Mrs. Glass broke in, her voice quiet but dangerous. "Oh, I'd like to put a diaper on that mouth of yours!"

"Well, gee whizz. I'm only trying to make polite bathroom talk."

"You're so *funny.* Oh, you're so funny! It just so *hap*pens, young man, that I don't consider your little sister in exactly the exact same light that I do the Lord. I may be pe*culi*ar, but I don't happen to. I don't happen to see any comparison whatsoever between the *Lord* and a rundown, overwrought little college girl that's been reading too many religious books and all like that! You certainly know your sister as well as I do—or *should*. She's *ter*ribly impressionable and always has been, and you know it very well!"

The bathroom was oddly still for a moment.

"Mother? Are you sitting down out there? I have a terrible feeling you're sitting down out there with about five cigarettes going. Are you?" He waited. Mrs. Glass, however, didn't choose to reply. "I *don't* want you sitting down out there, Bessie. I'd like to get out of this God-damned tub. . . . Bessie? You hear me?"

"I hear you, I hear you," Mrs. Glass said. A fresh wave of worry had passed over her face. She straightened her back restively. "She's got that crazy Bloomberg in bed with her on the couch," she said. "It isn't even *healthy*." She gave a mighty sigh. For several minutes she had been holding her cigarette ashes in her cupped left hand. She now reached over, without quite having to get up, and emptied them into the wastebasket. "I *don't* know what I'm supposed to do," she announced. "I just don't, that's all. The house is absolutely upside down. The painters are almost *fin*ished in her room, and they're going to want to get in the living room im*medi*ately after lunch. I don't know whether to wake her *up,* or what. She's had almost *no* sleep. I'm simply losing my mind. Do you know how long it's *been* since I've even been *free* to have the painters in this apartment? Nearly *twen*—"

"The painters! Ah! The dawn comes up. I forgot all about the painters. Listen, why haven't you asked them in here? There's *plenty* of room. What the hell kind of host will they think I am, not asking them into the bathroom when I'm—"

"Just be quiet a minute, young man. I'm thinking."

As if in obedience, Zooey abruptly put his washcloth to use. For quite a little interval, the faint swush of it was the only sound in the bathroom. Mrs. Glass, seated eight or ten feet away from the shower curtain, stared across the tiled floor at the blue bathmat alongside the tub. Her cigarette had burned down to the last half inch. She held it between the ends of two fingers of her right hand. Distinctly, her way of holding it tended to blow to some sort of literary hell one's first, strong (and still perfectly tenable) impression that an invisible Dubliner's shawl covered her shoulders. Not only were her fingers of an extraordinary length and shapeliness—such as, very generally speaking, one wouldn't have expected of a medium-stout woman's fingers—but they featured, as it were, a somewhat imperial-looking tremor; a deposed Balkan queen or a retired favorite courtesan might have had such an elegant tremor. And this was not the only contradiction to the Dublin-black-shawl motif. There was the rather eyebrow-raising fact of

Bessie Glass's legs, which were comely by any criterion. They were the legs of a once quite widely acknowledged public beauty, a vaudevillian, a dancer, a very light dancer. They were crossed now, as she sat staring at the bathmat, left over right, a worn white terrycloth slipper looking as if it might fall off the extended foot at any second. The feet were extraordinarily small, the ankles were still slender, and, perhaps most remarkable, the calves were still firm and evidently never had been knotty.

A much deeper sigh than customary—almost, it seemed, a part of the life force itself—suddenly came from Mrs. Glass. She got up and carried her cigarette over to the washbowl, let cold water run on it, then dropped the extinguished stub into the wastebasket and sat down again. The spell of introspection she had cast on herself was unbroken, as if she hadn't moved from her seat at all.

"I'm getting out of here in about three seconds, Bessie! I'm giving you fair warning. Let's not wear out our welcome, buddy."

Mrs. Glass, who had resumed staring at the blue bathmat, gave an absent-minded nod at this "fair warning." And at that instant, more than just mentionably, had Zooey seen her face, and particularly her eyes, he might have had a strong impulse, passing or not, to recall, or reconstruct, or reinflect the greater part of his share of the conversation that had passed between them—to temper it, to soften it. On the other hand, he might not have. It was a very touch-and-go business, in 1955, to get a wholly plausible reading from Mrs. Glass's face, and especially from her enormous blue eyes. Where once, a few years earlier, her eyes alone could break the news (either to people or to bathmats) that two of her sons were dead, one by suicide (her favorite, her most intricately calibrated, her kindest son), and one killed in World War II (her only truly lighthearted son)—where once Bessie Glass's eyes alone could report these facts, with an eloquence and a seeming passion for detail that neither her husband nor any of her adult surviving children could bear to look at, let alone take in, now, in 1955, she was apt to use this same terrible Celtic equipment to break the news, usually at the front door, that the new delivery boy hadn't brought the leg of lamb in time for dinner or that some remote Hollywood starlet's marriage was on the rocks.

She lit a fresh king-size cigarette abruptly, dragged on it, then stood up, exhaling smoke. "I'll be back in a minute," she said. The statement sounded, innocently, like a promise. "Just please use the bathmat when you get out," she added. "That's what it's there for." She left the bathroom, closing the door securely behind her.

It was rather as though, after being in makeshift wet dock for days, the Queen Mary had just sailed out of, say, Walden Pond, as suddenly and perversely as she had sailed in. Behind the shower curtain, Zooey closed his eyes for a few

seconds, as though his own small craft were listing precariously in the wake. Then he pulled
back the shower curtain and stared over at the
closed door. It was a weighty stare, and relief
was not really a great part of it. As much as anything else, it was the stare, not so paradoxically,
of a privacy-lover who, once his privacy has been
invaded, doesn't quite approve when the in-
vader just gets up and leaves, one-two-three, like
that.

NOT five minutes later, Zooey, with his hair
combed wet, stood barefoot at the washbowl,
wearing a pair of beltless dark-gray sharkskin
slacks, a face towel across his bare shoulders. A
pre-shaving ritual had already been put into effect. The window blind had been raised halfway; the bathroom door had been set ajar to let
the steam escape and clear the mirrors; a cigarette had been lit, dragged on, and placed within
easy reach on the frosted-glass ledge under the
medicine-cabinet mirror. At the moment, Zooey
had just finished squeezing lather cream onto
the end of a shaving brush. He put the tube of
lather, without re-capping it, somewhere into
the enamel background, out of his way. He
passed the flat of his hand squeakily back and
forth over the face of the medicine-cabinet mirror, wiping away most of the mist. Then he began to lather his face. His lathering technique
was very much out of the ordinary, although
identical in spirit with his actual shaving tech-

nique. That is, although he looked into the mirror while he lathered, he didn't watch where his brush was moving but, instead, looked directly into his own eyes, as though his eyes were neutral territory, a no man's land in a private war against narcissism he had been fighting since he was seven or eight years old. By now, when he was twenty-five, the little stratagem may well have been mostly reflexive, just as a veteran baseball player, at the plate, will tap his spikes with his bat whether he needs to or not. Nonetheless, a few minutes earlier, when he had combed his hair, he had done so with the very minimum amount of help from the mirror. And before that he had managed to dry himself in front of a full-length mirror without so much as glancing into it.

He had just finished lathering his face when his mother suddenly appeared in his shaving mirror. She stood in the doorway, a few feet behind him, one hand on the doorknob—a portrait of spurious hesitancy about making another full entrance into the room.

"Ah! What a pleasant and gracious surprise!" Zooey said into the mirror. "Come in, come in!" He laughed, or gave his roar, then opened the medicine cabinet and took down his razor.

Mrs. Glass advanced, meditatively. "Zooey..." she said. "I've been thinking." Her usual seating accommodation was directly at Zooey's left. She started to lower herself into place.

"Don't sit down! Let me drink you in first,"

Zooey said. Getting out of the tub, putting on his trousers, and combing his hair had apparently raised his spirits. "It isn't often we have visitors at our little chapel, and when we do, we try to make them feel—"

"Just be still a minute," Mrs. Glass said firmly, sitting. She crossed her legs. "I've been thinking. Do you think it would do any good to try to get hold of Waker? I *don't,* personally, but what do you think? I mean in my opinion what that child needs is a good psy*chi*atrist, not a priest or anything, but I may be *wrong.*"

"Oh, no. No, no. Not *wrong.* I've never known you to be *wrong,* Bessie. Your facts are always either untrue or exaggerated, but you're never *wrong*—no, no." With much delight, Zooey wet his razor and began to shave.

"Zooey, I'm *asking* you—just cut out the funny business, now, please. Do you or don't you think I should get in touch with Waker? I could call that Bishop Pinchot or whatever his name is, and he could probably tell me where I could at least *wire* him, if he's still on some crazy boat." Mrs. Glass reached out and drew the metal wastebasket in close to her and used it as an ashtray for the lighted cigarette she had brought in with her. "I *asked* Franny if she'd like to talk to him on the phone," she said. "*If* I could get hold of him."

Zooey rinsed his razor briefly. "What'd she say?" he asked.

Mrs. Glass adjusted her sitting position with

a little evasive shift to the right. "She *says* she doesn't want to talk to *any*body."

"Ah. We know better than that, don't we? We're not going to take a straight answer like that lying down, are we?"

"For your information, young man, I'm not going to take any answer of any kind from that child today," Mrs. Glass said, rallying. She addressed Zooey's lathered profile. "If you have a young girl lying in a room crying and *mum*bling to herself for forty-eight hours, you don't go to them for any *an*swers."

Zooey, without commenting, went on shaving.

"Answer my question, please. Do you or don't you think I should try to get in touch with Waker? I'm *afraid* to, frankly. He's so emotional —priest or no priest. If you tell Waker it looks like *rain*, his eyes all fill up."

Zooey shared his amusement at this remark with the reflection of his own eyes in the mirror. "There's hope for you yet, Bessie," he said.

"Well, if I can't get Buddy on the phone, and even *you* won't help, I'm going to have to do *some*thing," Mrs. Glass said. Looking vastly troubled, she sat smoking for a long moment. Then: "If it was something strictly Catholic, or like that, I might be able to help her myself. I haven't forgotten *ev*erything. But none of you children were brought *up* as Catholics, and I really don't see—"

Zooey cut her short. "You're off," he said,

turning his lathered face toward her. "You're off. You're way off. I told you that last night. This thing with Franny is strictly non-sectarian." He dipped his razor and continued to shave. "Just take my word, please."

Mrs. Glass stared full and pressingly at his profile, as if he might say something further, but he didn't. At length, she sighed, and said, "I'd *al*most be satisfied for a while if I could get that awful Bloomberg off that couch with her. It isn't even *san*itary." She dragged on her cigarette. "And I *don't* know what I'm supposed to do about the painters. This very minute they're practically finished in her room, and they're going to be champing at the *bit* to get in the living room."

"You know, I'm the only one in this family who has no problems," Zooey said. "And you know why? Because any time I'm feeling blue, or *puzzled,* what I do, I just invite a few people to come visit me in the bathroom, and—well, we iron things out together, that's all."

Mrs. Glass seemed on the point of being diverted by Zooey's method of dealing with problems, but it was her day to suppress all forms of amusement. She stared at him for a moment, and then, slowly, a new look gathered in her eyes—resourceful, crafty, and a trifle desperate. "You know, I'm not as stupid as you may think, young man," she said. "You're all so *sec*retive, all you children. It just so happens, if you must know, that I know more about what's behind all this than you think I do." For emphasis, lips compressed, she brushed some imaginary tobacco flakes from the lap of her kimono. "For your information, I happen to know that that little book she carried all around the whole house with her yesterday is at the whole *root* of this whole business."

Zooey turned and glanced at her. He was grinning. "How'd you figure that out?" he said.

"Just never *mind* how I figured it out," Mrs. Glass said. "If you must know, Lane has called up here *sev*eral times. He's *ter*ribly worried about Franny."

Zooey rinsed his razor. "Who in hell is Lane?" he asked. Unmistakably, it was the question of a still very young man who, now and then, is not inclined to admit that he knows the first names of certain people.

"You know very well who he is, young man," Mrs. Glass said with emphasis. "Lane Cou*tell*. He's only *been* Franny's boy friend for a whole year. You've met him at least half a dozen times that *I* know of, so just don't pretend you don't know who he is."

Zooey gave a genuine roar of laughter, as if he clearly relished seeing any affectation brought to light, his own included. He went on shaving, still delighted. "The expression is Franny's 'young man,'" he said, "not her 'boy friend.' Why are you so out of date, Bessie? Why is that? Hm?"

"Never mind why I'm so out of date. It may

[96]

interest you to know that he's called up here five or six times since Franny got home—twice this morning before you were even *up*. He's been very sweet, and he's terribly concerned and *worried* about Franny."

"Not like some people we know, eh? Well, I hate to disillusion you, but I've sat by the hour with him and he's not sweet at all. He's a charm boy and a fake. Incidentally, somebody around here's been shaving their armpits or their goddam legs with my razor. Or *dropped* it. The head's way out of—"

"Nobody's touched your razor, young man. Why is he a charm boy and a fake, may I ask?"

"Why? Because he is, that's all. Probably because it's paid off. I can tell you one thing. If he's worried about Franny at all, I'll lay odds it's for the crummiest reasons. He's *prob*ably worried because he minded leaving the goddam football game before it was over—worried because he probably showed he minded it and he knows Franny's sharp enough to have noticed. I can just picture the little bastard getting her into a cab and putting her on a train and wondering if he can make it back to the game before the half ended."

"Oh, it's impossible to talk to you! But absolutely impossible. I don't know why I try, even. You're just like Buddy. You think everybody does something for some pe*cu*liar *reas*on. You don't think anybody calls anybody else up without having some nasty, selfish *reas*on for it."

"Exactly—in nine cases out of ten. And this Lane pill isn't the exception, you can be sure. Listen, I talked with him for twenty deadly goddam minutes one night while Franny was getting ready to go out, and I say he's a big nothing." He reflected, arresting his razor stroke. "What in hell was it he was telling me? Something very *winning*. What was it? . . . Oh, yes. *Yes*. He was telling me he used to listen to Franny and me every week when he was a kid —and you know what he was doing, the little bastard? He was building *me* up at Franny's expense. For absolutely *no reason* except to ingratiate himself and show off his hot little Ivy League intellect." Zooey put out his tongue and gave a subdued, modified Bronx cheer. "Phooey," he said, and resumed using his razor. "Phooey, I say, on all white-shoe college boys who edit their campus literary magazines. Give me an honest con man any day."

Mrs. Glass directed a long and oddly comprehensive look at his profile. "He's a young boy not out of college yet. And you make people nervous, young man," she said—most equably, for her. "You either take to somebody or you don't. If you do, then you do all the talking and nobody can even get a word in edgewise. If you *don't* like somebody—which is most of the time —then you just sit around like death it*self* and let the person talk themselves into a hole. I've seen you do it."

Zooey turned full around to look at his mother.

He turned around and looked at her, in this instance, in precisely the same way that, at one
time or another, in one year or another, all his
brothers and sisters (and especially his brothers)
had turned around and looked at her. Not just
with objective wonder at the rising of a truth,
fragmentary or not, up through what often
seemed to be an impenetrable mass of preju-
dices, clichés, and bromides. But with admira-
tion, affection, and, not least, gratitude. And,
oddly or no, Mrs. Glass invariably took this
"tribute," when it came, in beautiful stride. She
would look back with grace and modesty at the
son or daughter who had given her the look. She
now presented this gracious and modest coun-
tenance to Zooey. "You do," she said, without
accusation in her voice. "Neither you nor Buddy
know how to talk to people you don't like."
She thought it over. "Don't love, really," she
amended. And Zooey continued to stand gazing
at her, not shaving. "It's not right," she said—
gravely, sadly. "You're getting so much like
Buddy used to be when he was your age. Even
your father's noticed it. If you don't like somebody in two minutes, you're done with them
forever." Mrs. Glass looked over, abstractedly,
at the blue bathmat, across the tiled floor. Zooey
stood as still as possible, in order not to break
her mood. "You can't live in the world with
such strong likes and dislikes," Mrs. Glass said
to the bathmat, then turned again toward Zooey
and gave him a long look, with very little, if

any, morality in it. "Regardless of what you may think, young man," she said.

Zooey looked back at her steadily, then smiled and faced around to examine his beard in the mirror. Mrs. Glass, watching him, sighed. She bent and put out her cigarette against the inside of the metal wastebasket. She lit a fresh cigarette almost at once, and said, as pointedly as she was able, "Anyway, your *sis*ter says he's a brilliant boy. Lane."

"That's just sex talking, buddy," Zooey said. "I know that voice. Oh, do I know that voice!" The last trace of lather had been shaved away from his face and throat. He felt his throat critically with one hand, then picked up his shaving brush and began to re-lather strategic parts of his face. "All right, what does Lane have to say on the phone?" he asked. "According to Lane, what's behind Franny's troubles?"

Mrs. Glass sat slightly and avidly forward, and said, "Well, *Lane* says it all has to do—this entire thing—with that little book she's got with her all the time. You know. That little book she kept reading all yesterday and dragging with her everywhere she—"

"I know that little book. Go on."

"Well, he says, Lane says, it's a terribly religious little book—fa*nat*ical and all like that— and that she got it out of the library at college and now she thinks maybe she's—" Mrs. Glass broke off. Zooey had turned toward her with somewhat menacing alertness. "What's the *matter*?" she asked.

"He said she got it where?"

"Out of the library. At college. Why?"

Zooey shook his head, and turned back to the washbowl. He put down his shaving brush and opened the medicine cabinet.

"What's the matter?" Mrs. Glass demanded. "What's the matter with that? Why such a look, young man?"

Zooey didn't reply till he had opened a new package of razor blades. Then, dismantling his razor, he said, "You're so stupid, Bessie." He ejected the blade from his razor.

"Why am I so stupid? Incidentally, you just *put* a new razor blade in yesterday."

Zooey, his face expressionless, locked a new blade into his razor and began his second-time-over shave.

"I asked you a question, young man. Why am I so stupid? *Didn't* she get that little book out of her college library, or what?"

"No, she didn't, Bessie," Zooey said, shaving. "That little book is called 'The Pilgrim Continues His Way,' and it's a sequel to another little book, called 'The Way of a Pilgrim,' which she's also dragging around with her, and she got *both* books out of Seymour and Buddy's old room, where they've been sitting on Seymour's desk for as long as I can remember. Jesus God almighty."

"Well, don't get abusive about it! Is it so *ter-*

rible to think she might have gotten them out of her college library and simply brought them—"

"Yes! It *is* terrible. It *is* terrible when both books have been sitting on Seymour's goddam desk for *years*. It's depressing."

An unexpected, a singularly noncombatant, note came into Mrs. Glass's voice. "I don't go in that room if I can help it, and you know it," she said. "I don't look at Seymour's old—at his things."

Zooey said, quickly, "All right, I'm sorry." Without looking at her, and although he hadn't quite finished his second-time-over shave, he pulled the face towel down from his shoulders and wiped the remaining lather off his face. "Let's just drop this for a while," he said, and tossed the face towel over onto the radiator; it landed on the title page of the Rick-Tina manuscript. He unscrewed his razor and held it under the cold-water tap.

His apology had been genuine, and Mrs. Glass knew it, but evidently she couldn't resist taking advantage of it, perhaps because of its rarity. "You're not kind," she said, watching him rinse his razor. "You're not kind at all, Zooey. You're old enough to at least try for some kind of kindness when you're feeling mean. Buddy, at least, when he's feeling—" She simultaneously took in her breath and gave a great start as Zooey's razor, new blade and all, slam-banged down into the metal wastebasket.

Quite probably Zooey hadn't intended to send

his razor crashing into the wastebasket but had merely brought his left hand down with such suddenness and violence that the razor got away from him. In any case, it was certain that he hadn't intended to strike and hurt his wrist on the side of the washbowl. "Buddy, Buddy, *Buddy,*" he said. "Seymour, Seymour, *Seymour.*" He had turned toward his mother, whom the crash of the razor had startled and alarmed but not really frightened. "I'm so sick of their names I could cut my throat." His face was pale but very nearly expressionless. "This whole goddam house stinks of ghosts. I don't mind so much being haunted by a dead ghost, but I resent like *hell* being haunted by a half-dead one. I wish to *God* Buddy'd make up his mind. He does everything else Seymour ever did—or tries to. Why the hell doesn't he kill himself and be done with it?"

Mrs. Glass blinked her eyes, just once, and Zooey instantly looked away from her face. He bent over and fished his razor out of the wastebasket. "We're *freaks,* the two of us, Franny and I," he announced, standing up. "I'm a twenty-five-year-old freak and she's a twenty-year-old freak, and both those bastards are responsible." He put his razor on the edge of the washbowl, but it slid obstreperously down into the bowl. He quickly picked it out, and this time kept it in the grasp of his fingers. "The symptoms are a little more delayed in Franny's case than mine, but she's a freak, too, and don't you forget it. I swear to you, I could murder them both without even batting an eyelash. The great teachers. The great emancipators. My God. I can't even sit down to lunch with a man any more and hold up my end of a decent conversation. I either get so bored or so goddam preachy that if the son of a bitch had any sense, he'd break his chair over my head." He suddenly opened the medicine cabinet. He stared rather vacuously into it for a few seconds, as though he had forgotten why he opened it, then put his undried razor in its place on one of the shelves.

Mrs. Glass sat very still, watching him, her cigarette burning low between her fingers. She watched him put the cap on the tube of shaving lather. He had some difficulty finding the thread.

"Not that anybody's interested, but I can't even sit down to a goddam *meal,* to this day, without first saying the Four Great Vows under my breath, and I'll lay any odds you want Franny can't, either. They drilled us with such goddam—"

"The four great what?" Mrs. Glass interrupted, but cautiously.

Zooey put a hand on each side of the washbowl and leaned his chest forward a trifle, his eyes on the general background of enamel. For all his slightness of body, he looked at that moment ready and able to push the washbowl straight through the floor. "The Four Great *Vows,*" he said, and, with rancor, closed his eyes. " 'However in*num*erable beings are, I vow to

save them; however inexh*aust*ible the passions
are, I vow to extinguish them; however immeas-
urable the Dharmas are, I vow to master them;
however incomparable the Buddha-truth is, I vow
to *attain* it.' Yay, team. I know I can do it. Just
put me in, coach." His eyes stayed closed. "My
God, I've been mumbling that under my breath
three meals a day every day of my life since I
was ten. I can't *eat* unless I say it. I tried skip-
ping it once when I was having a lunch with
LeSage. I gagged on a goddam cherrystone clam,
doing it." He opened his eyes, frowned, but kept
his peculiar stance. "How 'bout getting out of
here, now, Bessie?" he said. "I mean it. Lemme
finish my goddam ablutions in peace, please."
His eyes closed again, and he appeared ready
to have another try at pushing the washbowl
through the floor. Even though his head was
slightly down, a considerable amount of blood
had flowed out of his face.

"I wish you'd get married," Mrs. Glass said,
abruptly, wistfully.

Everyone in the Glass family—Zooey certainly
not least—was familiar with this sort of non-
sequitur from Mrs. Glass. It bloomed best, most
sublimely, in the middle of an emotional flareup
of just this kind. This time, it caught Zooey very
much off guard, however. He gave an explosive
sound, mostly through the nose, of either laughter or the opposite of laughter. Mrs. Glass quickly
and anxiously leaned forward to see which it
was. It was laughter, more or less, and she sat

back, relieved. "Well, I *do*," she insisted. "Why *don't* you?"

Relaxing his stance, Zooey took a folded linen handkerchief from his hip pocket, flipped it open, then used it to blow his nose once, twice, three times. He put away the handkerchief, saying, "I like to ride in trains too much. You never get to sit next to the window any more when you're married."

"That's no reason!"

"It's a perfect reason. Go away, Bessie. Leave me in peace in here. Why don't you go for a nice elevator ride? You're going to burn your fingers, incidentally, if you don't put out that goddam cigarette."

Mrs. Glass put out her cigarette against the inside of the wastebasket again. She then sat quietly for a little interval, without reaching for her cigarette pack and matches. She watched Zooey take down a comb and re-part his hair. "You could use a *hair*cut, young man," she said. "You're getting to look like one of these crazy Hun*gar*ians or something getting out of a *swim*ming pool."

Zooey perceptibly smiled, went on for a few seconds with his combing, then suddenly turned. He wagged his comb briefly at his mother. "One other thing. Before I forget. And *listen* to me, now, Bessie," he said. "If you get any more ideas, like last night, of phoning Philly Byrnes' goddam psychoanalyst for Franny, just do one thing—that's all I ask. Just think of what analysis did for Seymour." He paused for emphasis. "Hear me? Will you do that?"

Mrs. Glass immediately gave her hairnet an unnecessary adjustment, then took out her cigarettes and matches, but she merely kept them for a moment in her hand. "For your information," she said, "I didn't say I was *going* to phone Philly Byrnes' psychoanalyst, I said I was *think*ing about it. In the *first* place, he isn't just an ordinary psychoanalyst. He happens to be a *very* devout *Cath*olic psychoanalyst, and I thought it *might* be better than sitting around and watching that child—"

"Bessie, I'm warning you, now, God damn it. I don't care if he's a very devout Buddhist veterinarian. If you call in some—"

"There's no need for sarcasm, young man. I've known Philly Byrnes since he was a tiny little *boy*. Your father and I played on the same *bill* with his parents for *years*. And I happen to know for a fact that going to a psychoanalyst has made an absolutely *new* and *lovely* person out of that boy. I was talking to his—"

Zooey slammed his comb into the medicine cabinet, then impatiently flipped the cabinet door shut. "Oh, you're so stupid, Bessie," he said. "Philly *Byrnes*. Philly Byrnes is a poor little impotent sweaty guy past *forty* who's been sleeping for years with a rosary and a copy of *Variety* under his pillow. We're talking about two things as different as day and night. Now, listen to me, Bessie." Zooey turned full toward his mother and looked at her carefully, the flat of one hand on the enamel, as if for support. "You listening to me?"

Mrs. Glass finished lighting a fresh cigarette before she committed herself. Then, exhaling smoke and brushing off imaginary tobacco flakes from her lap, she said grimly, "I'm listening to you."

"All right. I'm *very* serious, now. If you— Listen to me, now. If you can't, or won't, think of Seymour, then you go right ahead and call in some ignorant psychoanalyst. You just do that. You just call in some analyst who's experienced in adjusting people to the joys of television, and *Life* magazine every Wednesday, and European travel, and the H-Bomb, and Presidential elections, and the front page of the *Times,* and the responsibilities of the Westport and Oyster Bay Parent-Teacher Association, and God knows what else that's gloriously normal—you just *do* that, and I swear to you, in not more than a year Franny'll either be in a *nut* ward or she'll be wandering off into some goddam desert with a burning cross in her hands."

Mrs. Glass brushed off a few more imaginary tobacco flakes. "All right, all right—don't get so *upset,*" she said. "For goodness' sake. Nobody's called anybody."

Zooey yanked open the door of the medicine cabinet, stared inside, then took down a nail file and closed the door. He picked up the cigarette he had posted on the edge of the frosted-glass ledge and dragged on it, but it was dead. His mother said, "Here," and handed him her pack of king-size cigarettes and her match folder.

Zooey took a cigarette out of the pack and got as far as putting it between his lips and striking a match, but the pressure of thoughts made the actual lighting of the cigarette unfeasible, and he blew out the match and took the cigarette down from his mouth. He gave a little, impatient headshake. "I don't know," he said. "It seems to me there *must* be a psychoanalyst holed up somewhere in town who'd be good for Franny—I thought about that last night." He grimaced slightly. "But I don't happen to know of any. For a psychoanalyst to be any good with Franny at all, he'd have to be a pretty peculiar type. I don't know. He'd have to believe that it was through the grace of God that he'd been inspired to study psychoanalysis in the first place. He'd have to believe that it was through the grace of God that he wasn't run over by a goddam truck before he ever even got his license to practice. He'd have to believe that it's through the grace of God that he has the native intelligence to be able to help his goddam patients at *all*. I don't know any *good* analysts who think along those lines. But that's the only kind of psychoanalyst who might be able to do Franny any good at all. If she got somebody terribly Freudian, or terribly eclectic, or just terribly run-of-the-mill—somebody who didn't even have any crazy, mysterious *grat*itude for his insight

and intelligence—she'd come out of analysis in
even worse shape than Seymour did. It worried
hell out of me, thinking about it. Let's just shut
up about it, if you don't mind." He took time
to get his cigarette lighted. Then, exhaling
smoke, he put the cigarette up on the frosted-
glass ledge where the old, dead cigarette was,
and assumed a slightly more relaxed stance. He
began to run the nail file under his fingernails
—which were already perfectly clean. "If you
don't yak at me," he said, after a pause, "I'll tell
you what those two little books are about that
Franny's got with her. Are you interested, or
not? If you're not interested, I don't feel like—"

"*Yes,* I'm interested! Of *course* I'm interested! What do you think I'm—"

"All right, just don't yak at me for a minute,
then," Zooey said, and rested the small of his
back against the edge of the washbowl. He went
on using the nail file. "Both books are about a
Russian peasant, around the turn of the century," he said, in what was, for his implacably
matter-of-fact voice, a rather narrative tone.
"He's a very simple, very sweet little guy with a
withered arm. Which, of course, makes him a
natural for Franny, with that goddam Bide-a-
Wee Home heart of hers." He pivoted around,
picked up his cigarette from the frosted-glass
ledge, dragged on it, then began to file his nails.
"In the beginning, the little peasant tells you,
he had a wife and a farm. But he had a looney
brother who burned down the farm—and then,

later, I think, the wife just died. Anyway, he starts on his pilgrimage. And he has a problem. He's been reading the Bible all his life, and he wants to know what it means when it says, in Thessalonians, 'Pray without ceasing.' That one line keeps haunting him." Zooey reached for his cigarette again, dragged on it, and then said, "There's another, similar line in Timothy—'I will therefore that men pray everywhere.' And Christ himself, as a matter of fact, says, 'Men ought always to pray and not to faint.' " Zooey used his nail file in silence for a moment, his face singularly dour in expression. "So, anyway, he begins his pilgrimage to find a teacher," he said. "Someone who can teach him *how* to pray incessantly, and *why*. He walks and he walks and he walks, from one church and shrine to another, talking to this priest and that. Till finally he meets a simple old monk who apparently knows what it's all about. The old monk tells him that the one prayer acceptable to God at all times, and 'desired' by God, is the Jesus Prayer —'Lord Jesus Christ, have mercy on me.' *Actu*ally, the whole prayer is 'Lord Jesus Christ, have mercy on me, a miserable sinner,' but none of the adepts in either of the Pilgrim books put any emphasis—thank *God*—on the miserable-sinner part. Anyway, the old monk explains to him what will happen if the prayer is said incessantly. He gives him some practice sessions with it and sends him home. *And*—to make a long story short—after a while the little pilgrim becomes proficient with the prayer. He masters it. He's overjoyed with his new spiritual life, and he goes on hiking all over Russia—through dense forests, through towns, villages, and so on —saying his prayer as he goes along and telling everyone he happens to meet how to say it, too." Zooey looked up, brusquely, at his mother. "You listening to this? You fat old Druid?" he inquired. "Or are you just staring at my gorgeous face?"

Mrs. Glass, bristling, said, "Certainly I'm listening!"

"All right—I don't want any party poops around here." Zooey gave a great guffaw, then took a drag on his cigarette. He kept the cigarette stationed between his fingers and went on using the nail file. "The first of the two little books, 'The Way of a Pilgrim,' " he said, "has mostly to do with the adventures the little pilgrim has on the road. Whom he meets, what he says to them, what they say to him—he meets some goddam nice people, incidentally. The sequel, 'The Pilgrim Continues His Way,' is mostly a dissertation in dialogue form on the whys and wherefores of the Jesus Prayer. The pilgrim, a professor, a monk, and some sort of hermit all meet and hash over things. And that's all there is to it, really." Zooey glanced up, very briefly, at his mother, then switched the nail file over to his left hand. "The aim of *both* little books, if you're interested," he said, "is supposedly to wake everybody up to the need and *ben*efits of saying the Jesus Prayer incessantly. First under the supervision of a qualified teacher—a sort of Christian guru—and then, after the person's mastered it to some extent, he's supposed to go on with it on his own. And the main idea is that it's not supposed to be just for pious bastards and breast-beaters. You can be busy robbing the goddam poor box, but you're to say the prayer while you rob it. Enlightenment's supposed to come *with* the prayer, not before it." Zooey frowned, but academically. "The idea, really, is that sooner or later, completely on its own, the prayer moves from the lips and the head down to a center in the heart and becomes an automatic function in the person, right along with the heartbeat. And then, after a time, once the prayer *is* automatic in the heart, the person is supposed to enter into the so-called reality of things. The subject doesn't really come up in either of the books, but, in Eastern terms, there are seven subtle centers in the body, called *chakras,* and the one most closely connected with the heart is called *anahata,* which is supposed to be sensitive and powerful as hell, and when it's activated, it, in turn, activates another of these centers, between the eyebrows, called *ajna*—it's the pineal gland, really, or, rather, an aura around the pineal gland — and then, bingo, there's an opening of what mystics call the 'third eye.' It's nothing new, for God's sake. It didn't just start with the little pilgrim's crowd, I mean. In India, for God knows how many centuries, it's been known as *japam*. *Japam* is just the repetition of any of the human names of God. Or the names of his incarnations—his avatars, if you want to get technical. The idea being that if you call out the name long enough and regularly enough and *lit*erally from the heart, sooner or later you'll get an answer. Not exactly an *an*swer. A *response*." Zooey suddenly turned around, opened the medicine cabinet, replaced his nail file, and took down a remarkably stubby-looking orange stick. "Who's been eating my orange stick?" he said. With his wrist, he briefly blotted his perspiring upper lip, and then he began to use the orange stick to push back his cuticles.

Mrs. Glass took a deep drag on her cigarette, watching him, then crossed her legs and asked, demanded, "Is that what Franny's supposed to be doing? I mean is that what she's doing and all?"

"So I gather. Don't ask me, ask *her*."

There was a short pause, and a dubious one. Then Mrs. Glass abruptly and rather pluckily asked, "How long do you have to do it?"

Zooey's face lit up with pleasure. He turned to her. "How long?" he said. "Oh, not long. Till the painters want to get in your room. Then a procession of saints and bodhisattvas march in, carrying bowls of chicken broth. The Hall Johnson Choir starts up in the background, and the cameras move in on a nice old gentleman in a loincloth standing against a background of mountains and blue skies and white clouds, and a look of peace comes over everybody's—"

"All right, just *stop* that," Mrs. Glass said.

"Well, Jesus. I'm only trying to help. Mercy. I don't want you to go away with the impression that there're any—you know—any incon-*ven*iences involved in the religious life. I mean a lot of people don't take it up just because they think it's going to involve a certain amount of nasty application and perseverance—you know what I mean." It was clear that the speaker, with patent relish, was now reaching the high point of his address. He wagged his orange stick solemnly at his mother. "As soon as we get out of the chapel here, I hope you'll accept from me a little volume I've always admired. I believe it touches on some of the fine points we've discussed this morning. 'God Is My Hobby.' By Dr. Homer Vincent Claude Pierson, Jr. In this little book, I think you'll find, Dr. Pierson tells us very clearly how when he was twenty-one years of age he started putting aside a little time each day—two minutes in the morning and two minutes at night, if I remember correctly—and at the end of the *first year*, just by these little informal visits with God, he increased his annual income seventy-four per cent. I believe I have an extra copy, and if you'll be good enough—"

"Oh, you're impossible," Mrs. Glass said. But vaguely. Her eyes had again sought out her old friend the blue bathmat, across the room. She sat staring at it while Zooey—grinning but perspiring freely at his upper lip—went on using his orange stick. At length, Mrs. Glass heaved one of her premium sighs and returned her attention to Zooey, who, pushing at his cuticles, had pivoted a half turn toward the morning daylight. As she took in the lines and planes of his uncommonly spare unclothed back, her gaze gradually de-abstracted. In a matter of only a few seconds, in fact, her eyes appeared to jettison everything that was dark and heavy and to glow with fan-club appreciation. "You're getting so broad and lovely," she said, aloud, and reached out to touch the small of his back. "I was afraid all those crazy bar-bell exercises would do some—"

"*Don't*, willya?" Zooey said, quite sharply, recoiling.

"Don't *what?*"

Zooey pulled open the medicine-cabinet door and put the orange stick back in its niche. "Just don't, that's all. Don't admire my goddam back," he said, and closed the cabinet. He picked off a pair of black silk socks that were hanging on the towel bar and carried them over to the radiator. He sat down on the radiator, despite the heat— or because of it—and began to put on his socks.

Mrs. Glass gave a rather delayed snort. "Don't admire your back—I love that!" she said. But she was insulted, and a trifle hurt. She watched him put on his socks, with a mixed expression of injury and the ungovernable interest of someone who has been examining laundered socks for holes for a great many years. Then, suddenly, with one of her most audible sighs, she stood up and, grim and duty-bound, moved into the washstand area Zooey had vacated. Her first, blatantly martyred chore was to turn on the cold-water tap. "I wish you'd learn to put the caps back on things properly when you're finished using them," she said in a tone she fully meant to sound captious.

From the radiator, where he was attaching supporters to his socks, Zooey glanced up at her. "I wish you'd learn to leave the goddam party when it's over," he said. "I mean it, now, Bessie. I'd like about one minute of solitude in here— *rude* as it may sound. In the first place, I'm in a hurry. I have to be at LeSage's office at two-thirty, and I'd *like* to get a couple of things done downtown first. Let's go, now—do you mind?"

Mrs. Glass turned from her char duties to look at him and to ask a question of the kind that, over the years, had irritated every one of her children: "You're going to have some *lunch* before you go, aren't you?"

"I'll get a bite downtown. . . . Where the hell's my other shoe?"

Mrs. Glass stared at him, deliberately. "Are you or aren't you going to speak to your sister before you leave here?" she demanded.

"I don't *know*, Bessie," Zooey answered, after a perceptible hesitation. "Just stop asking me that, please. If I had something really hot to say to her this morning, I would. Just stop asking me." One shoe on and tied, the other shoe missing, he suddenly got down on his hands and knees and passed a hand back and forth under the radiator. "Ah. There you are, you little bastard," he said. A small bathroom scale stood beside the radiator. He sat down on it, missing shoe in hand.

Mrs. Glass watched him pull it on. She didn't stay for the tying of the lace, however. Instead, she left the room. But slowly. Moving with a certain uncharacteristic heaviness—a drag, actually—that distracted Zooey. He looked up and over at her with considerable attention. "I just don't know any more what's happened to all you children," Mrs. Glass said vaguely, without turning around. She stopped at one of the towel bars and straightened a washcloth. "In the old radio days, when you were all little and all, you all used to be so—smart and happy and—just *lovely*. Morning, noon, and night." She bent over and picked up from the tiled floor what appeared to be a long, mysteriously blondish human hair. She made a slight detour with it over to the wastebasket, saying, "I don't know what good it is to know so much and be smart as whips and all if it doesn't make you happy." Her back was toward Zooey as she moved again toward the door. "At least," she said, "you all used to be so sweet and loving to each other it was a joy to see." She opened the door, shaking her head. "Just a joy," she said firmly, and closed the door behind her.

Zooey, looking over at the closed door, inhaled deeply and exhaled slowly. "Some exit lines you give yourself, buddy!" he called after her—but only when he must have been sure that his voice wouldn't really reach her down the hall.

THE Glasses' living room was about as unready to have its walls repainted as a room can be. Franny Glass lay asleep on the couch, with an afghan over her; the "wall-to-wall" carpet had been neither taken up nor folded in at the borders; and the furniture—seemingly, a small warehouse of it—was in its usual static-dynamic distribution. The room was not impressively large, even by Manhattan apartment-house standards, but its accumulated furnishings might have lent a snug appearance to a banquet hall in Valhalla. There was a Steinway grand piano (invariably kept open), three radios (a 1927 Freshman, a 1932 Stromberg-Carlson, and a 1941 R.C.A.), a twenty-one-inch-screen television set, four table-model phonographs (including a 1920 Victrola, with its speaker still mounted intact, topside), cigarette and magazine tables galore, a regulation-size ping-pong table (mercifully collapsed and stored behind the piano), four comfortable chairs, eight uncomfortable chairs, a twelve-gallon tropical-fish tank (filled to capacity, in every sense of the word, and illuminated by two forty-watt bulbs), a love seat, the couch Franny was occupying, two empty bird cages, a cherrywood writing table, and an assortment of floor lamps, table lamps, and "bridge" lamps that sprang up all over the congested inscape like sumac. A cordon of waist-high bookcases lined three walls, their shelves cram-jammed and literally sagging with books—children's books, textbooks, second-hand books, Book Club books, plus an even more heterogeneous overflow from less communal "annexes" of the apartment. ("Dracula" now stood next to "Elementary Pali," "The Boy Allies at the Somme" stood next to "Bolts of Melody," "The Scarab Murder Case" and "The Idiot" were together, "Nancy Drew and the Hidden Staircase" lay on top of "Fear and Trembling.") Even if a resolute and unusually stout-hearted team of painters had been able to deal with the bookcases, the walls themselves, directly behind them, might well have made any self-respecting artisan turn in his union card. From the top of the bookcases to within less than a foot of the ceiling, the plaster —a blistery Wedgwood blue, where visible— was almost completely covered with what may very loosely be called "hangings," meaning a collection of framed photographs, yellowing personal and Presidential correspondence, bronze and silver plaques, and a sprawling miscellany of vaguely citational-looking documents and trophylike objects of various shapes and sizes, all attesting, one way or another, to the redoubtable fact that from 1927 through most of 1943 the network radio program called "It's a Wise Child" had very rarely gone on the air without one (and, more often, two) of the seven Glass children among its panelists. (Buddy Glass, who, at thirty-six, was the program's oldest living ex-panelist, not infrequently referred to the walls of his parents' apartment as being a kind of visual hymn to commercial American childhood and early puberty. He often expressed regret that his visits in from the country were so few and far between, and pointed out, usually at enormous length, how much luckier his brothers and sisters were, most of whom still lived in or around New York City.) The decoration scheme for the walls was, in fact, the brain child—with Mrs. Glass's unreserved spiritual sanction and everlastingly withheld formal consent—of Mr. Les Glass, the children's father, a former inter-national vaudevillian and, no doubt, an invete-rate and wistful admirer of the wall décor at Sardi's theatrical restaurant. Mr. Glass's perhaps most inspired coup as a decorator was manifest just behind and above the couch where young Franny Glass was now sleeping. There, in almost incestuously close juxtaposition, seven scrap-books of newspaper and magazine clippings had been bracketed, at the bindings, directly into the plaster. Year after year, plainly, all seven scrapbooks stood ready to be perused or pored over by old close friends of the family and casual visitors .alike, as well as, presumably, the odd part-time cleaning woman.

Just mentionably, Mrs. Glass had managed earlier that morning to make two token gestures on behalf of the arriving painters. The room could be entered through either the hall or the

dining room, and at each of these entrances there
were glass-paned double doors. Directly after
breakfast, Mrs. Glass had stripped the doors of
their pleated silk curtains. And later, at an op-
portune moment, when Franny was pretending
to sample a cup of chicken broth, Mrs. Glass had
climbed up on the window seats with the agility
of a mountain nanny goat and stripped all three
of the sash windows of their heavy damask curtains.

The room had a single, a southern, exposure.
A four-story private school for girls stood directly across the side street—a stolid and rather
aloofly anonymous-looking building that rarely
came alive till about three-thirty in the afternoon, when public-school children from Third
and Second Avenues came to play jacks or stoop-
ball on its stone steps. The Glasses had a fifth-
story apartment, a story higher than the school
building, and at this hour the sun was shining
over the school roof and through the Glasses'
naked living-room windows. Sunshine was very
unkind to the room. Not only were the furnishings old, intrinsically unlovely, and clotted with
memory and sentiment, but the room itself in
past years had served as the arena for countless
hockey and football (tackle as well as "touch")
games, and there was scarcely a leg on any piece
of furniture that wasn't badly nicked or marred.
There were scars much nearer to eye level, too,
from a rather awesome variety of airborne objects—beanbags, baseballs, marbles, skate keys,

soap erasers, and even, on one well-marked occasion in the early nineteen-thirties, a flying headless porcelain doll. Sunshine, however, was perhaps most particularly unkind to the carpet. It had originally been a port-red color—and by lamplight, at least, still was—but it now featured a number of rather pancreas-shaped faded spots, unsentimental mementos, all, of a series of household pets. The sun at this hour shone as far, as deep, as mercilessly into the room as the television set, striking it squarely in its unblinking cyclopean eye.

Mrs. Glass, who did some of her most inspired, most perpendicular thinking on the threshold of linen closets, had bedded down her youngest child on the couch between pink percale sheets, and covered her with a pale-blue cashmere afghan. Franny now lay sleeping on her left side, facing into the back of the couch and the wall, her chin just grazing one of the several toss pillows all around her. Her mouth was closed, but only just. Her right hand, however, on the coverlet, was not merely closed but shut tight; the fingers were clenched, the thumb tucked in—it was as though, at twenty, she had checked back into the mute, fisty defenses of the nursery. And here at the couch, it should be mentioned, the sun, for all its ungraciousness to the rest of the room, was behaving beautifully. It shone full on Franny's hair, which was jet-black and very prettily cut, and had been washed three times in as many days. Sunshine, in fact, bathed the entire afghan, and the play of warm, brilliant light in the pale-blue wool was in itself well worth beholding.

Zooey, almost direct from the bathroom, with a lighted cigar in his mouth, stood for quite a while at the foot of the couch, at first busy tucking in the ends of a white shirt he had put on, then buttoning his cuffs, and then merely standing and looking. He wore a frown behind his cigar, as though the stunning lighting effects had been "created" by a stage director whose taste he considered more or less suspect. Despite the extraordinary fineness of his features, and his age, and his general stature—clothed, he could easily have passed for a young, underweight *danseur* —the cigar was not markedly unbecoming to him. For one reason, he was not really short-nosed. For another, cigars, with Zooey, were not in any patent way a young man's affectation. He had been smoking them since he was sixteen, and regularly, as many as a dozen a day —expensive panatelas, for the most part—since he was eighteen.

A Vermont-marble coffee table, rectangular and quite long, stood parallel and very close to the couch. Zooey abruptly went over to it. He moved an ashtray, a silver cigarette box, and a copy of *Harper's Bazaar* out of the way, then directly sat down in the narrow space on the cold marble surface, facing—almost hovering over— Franny's head and shoulders. He looked briefly at the clenched hand on the blue afghan, then,

quite gently, with his cigar in his hand, took
hold of Franny's shoulder. "Franny," he said.
"Frances. Let's go, buddy. Let's not fritter away
the best part of the day here. . . . Let's go,
buddy."

Franny awakened with a start—a jolt, really,
as though the couch had just gone over a bad
bump. She raised up on one arm, and said,
"Whew." She squinted at the morning sunlight.
"Why's it so sunny?" She only partly took in
Zooey's presence. "Why's it so sunny?" she repeated.

Zooey observed her rather narrowly. "I bring
the sun wherever I go, buddy," he said.

Franny, still squinting, stared at him. "Why'd
you wake me up?" she asked. She was still too
heavy with sleep to sound really fractious, but it
was apparent that she felt there was some kind
of injustice in the air.

"Well . . . it's like this. Brother Anselmo and
I have been offered a new parish. In Labrador,
see. And we wondered if you'd give us your
blessing before we—"

"Whew!" Franny said again, and put her hand
on top of her head. Her hair, cut fashionably
short, had survived sleep very well indeed. She
wore it—most fortunately for the viewer—
parted in the middle. "Oh, I had the most horrible dream," she said. She sat up a bit and, with
one hand, closed the lapels of her dressing gown.
It was a tailored tie-silk dressing gown, beige,
with a pretty pattern of minute pink tea roses.

"Go ahead," Zooey said, dragging on his cigar. "I'll interpret for you."

She shuddered. "It was just horrible. So *spidery*. I've never had such a spidery nightmare in my entire life."

"Spiders, eh? That's very interesting. Very significant. I had a very interesting case in Zurich, some years back—a young person very much like yourself, as a matter of fact—"

"Be quiet a second, or I'll forget it," Franny said. She stared avidly into space, as nightmare-recallers do. There were half circles under her eyes, and other, subtler signs that mark an acutely troubled young girl, but nonetheless no one could have missed seeing that she was a first-class beauty. Her skin was lovely, and her features were delicate and most distinctive. Her eyes were very nearly the same quite astonishing shade of blue as Zooey's, but were set farther apart, as a sister's eyes no doubt should be—and they were not, so to speak, a day's work to look into, as Zooey's were. Some four years earlier, at her graduation from boarding school, her brother Buddy had morbidly prophesied to himself, as she grinned at him from the graduates' platform, that she would in all probability one day marry a man with a hacking cough. So there was *that* in her face, too. "Oh, God, I remember it now!" she said. "It was just hideous. I was at a *swim*ming pool somewhere, and a whole bunch of people kept making me dive for a can of Medaglia d'Oro coffee that was on the bottom.

Every time I'd come up, they'd make me go down again. I was crying, and I kept saying to everybody, '*You* have your bathing suits on. Why don't you do a little diving, too?,' but they'd all just laugh and make these terribly snide little remarks, and down I'd go again." She gave another shudder. "These two girls that are in my dorm were there. Stephanie Logan, and a girl I hardly even *know*—somebody, as a matter of fact, I always felt terribly *sorry* for, because she had such an awful name. Sharmon Sherman. They both had a big oar, and they kept trying to *hit* me with it every time I'd surface." Franny put her hands over her eyes briefly. "Whew!" She shook her head. She reflected. "The only person that made any *sense* in the dream was Professor Tupper. I mean he was the only person that was there that I *know* really detests me."

"Detests you, eh? Very interesting." Zooey's cigar was in his mouth. He revolved it slowly between his fingers, like a dream-interpreter who isn't getting all the facts in the case. He looked very contented. "Why does he detest you?" he asked. "Without absolute frankness, you realize, my hands are—"

"He detests me because I'm in this crazy Religion seminar he conducts, and I can never bring myself to smile back at him when he's being charming and Oxfordish. He's on lend-*lease* or something from Oxford, and he's just a terribly sad old self-satisfied phony with wild and woolly white hair. I think he goes into the men's room and musses it up before he comes to class—I honestly do. He has no enthusiasm whatever for his subject. Ego, yes. Enthusiasm, no. Which would be all right—I mean it wouldn't be anything exactly *strange*—but he keeps dropping idiotic hints that he's a *Realized Man* himself and we should be pretty happy kids to have him in this country." Franny grimaced. "The only thing he does with any *zing*, when he isn't bragging, is correct somebody when they say something's Sanskrit when it's really Pali. He just *knows* I can't stand him! You should see the faces I make at him when he isn't looking."

"What was he doing at the pool?"

"That's exactly it! Nothing! Absolutely nothing! He was just standing around smiling and *watch*ing. He was the worst one there."

Zooey, looking at her through his cigar smoke, said dispassionately, "You look like hell. You know that?"

Franny stared at him. "You could have sat there all morning without saying that," she said. She added, with meaning, "Just don't start in on me again, bright and early in the morning, Zooey, please. I mean it, now."

"Nobody's starting in on you, buddy," Zooey said, in the same dispassionate tone. "You just happen to look like hell, that's all. Why don't you eat something? Bessie says she's got some chicken soup out there she's—"

"If anybody else mentions chicken soup to me just once more—"

Zooey's attention, however, had been diverted. He was looking down at the sun-bathed afghan where it covered Franny's calves and ankles. "Who's that?" he said. "Bloomberg?" He put out a finger and gently poked a rather large and oddly mobile-looking bulge under the afghan. "Bloomberg? That you?"

The bulge stirred. Franny had her eye on it now, too. "I can't get rid of him," she said. "He's suddenly become absolutely *mad* about me."

Under the stimulus of Zooey's investigating finger, Bloomberg abruptly stretched, then began to tunnel slowly up toward the open country of Franny's lap. The instant his unprepossessing head emerged into daylight, sunlight, Franny took him under the shoulders and lifted him up into intimate greeting distance. "Good *morn*ing, Bloomberg dear!" she said, and kissed him fervently between the eyes. He blinked with aversion. "Good *morn*ing, old fat smelly cat. Good morning, good morning, good morning!" She gave him kiss after kiss, but no reciprocal waves of affection rose from him. He made an inept and rather violent attempt to cross over to Franny's collarbone. He was a very large mottled-gray "altered" tomcat. "Isn't he being af*fec*tionate?" Franny marvelled. "I've never *seen* him so affectionate." She looked at Zooey, possibly for corroboration, but Zooey's expres-

sion, behind his cigar, was noncommittal. "Pet
him, Zooey! Look how sweet he looks. *Pet* him."

Zooey put out a hand and stroked Bloomberg's arched back, once, twice, then quit, and
got up from the coffee table and meandered
across the room to the piano. It stood, in profile,
wide open, in all its black, Steinway enormity,
opposite the couch, its bench almost directly
across from Franny. Zooey sat down on the
bench, tentatively, then looked with very apparent interest at the sheet music on the stand.

"He's so full of fleas it isn't even funny,"
Franny said. She grappled briefly with Bloom-
berg, trying to coerce him into a docile lap-cat's
repose. "I found fourteen fleas on him last night.
Just on one side." She gave Bloomberg's hips a
mighty, downward push, then looked over at
Zooey. "How was the script, anyway?" she asked.
"Did it come last night finally, or what?"

Zooey didn't answer her. "My God," he said,
still looking at the sheet music on the stand.
"Who took this out?" The sheet music was entitled "You Needn't Be So Mean, Baby." It was
about forty years old. A sepia reproduction of
Mr. and Mrs. Glass was featured on the cover.
Mr. Glass was wearing a top hat and tails, and
so was Mrs. Glass. They were smiling rather
brilliantly at the camera, both of them leaning
forward on their evening canes, feet wide apart.

"What is it?" Franny asked. "I can't see."

"Bessie and Les. 'You Needn't Be So Mean,
Baby.' "

"Oh." Franny giggled. "Les was Reminiscing last night. For my benefit. He thinks I have a stomachache. He took out every single sheet of music in the whole bench."

"I'd be interested to know just how in hell we ever landed in this goddam jungle, all the way from 'You Needn't Be So Mean, Baby.' You figure it out."

"I can't. I've tried," Franny said. "How was the script? Did it come? You said Whosis—Mr. LeSage or whatever his name is—was going to drop it off with the doorman before he—"

"It came, it came," Zooey said. "I don't care to discuss it." He put his cigar in his mouth, and, with his right hand, up in the treble keys, he began to play, in octaves, the melody of a song called "The Kinkajou," which, somewhat notably, had shifted into and ostensibly out of popularity before he was born. "Not only *it* came," he said, "but Dick Hess called up here about one o'clock last night—just after *our* little fracas—and asked me to meet him for a drink, the bastard. At the San Remo, yet. He's discovering the Village. God almighty!"

"Don't bang the piano keys," Franny said, watching him. "I'll be your director if you're going to sit there. That's my first direction. Don't bang the piano keys."

"*First* of all, he knows I don't drink. Second, he knows I was born in New York and that if there's one thing I can't stand it's *at*mosphere. Third, he knows I live about seventy goddam blocks from the Village. And *fourth,* I told him three times I was in my pajamas and slippers."

"Don't bang the keys," Franny directed, petting Bloomberg.

"But *no,* it couldn't wait. He had to see me right away. Very important. No kidding, now. Be a good guy for *once* in your life and hop in a cab and c'mon down."

"Did you? Don't bang the lid down, either. That's my second—"

"Yes, *cer*tainly I did! I have no goddam will power!" Zooey said. He closed the keyboard lid, impatiently but without banging it. "The trouble with me is, I don't trust any out-of-towners in New York. I don't care how the hell long they've been here. I'm always afraid they're going to get run over, or beaten *up,* while they're busy discovering some little Armenian restaurant on Second Avenue. Or some damn thing." Morosely, he blew a stream of cigar smoke over the top of "You Needn't Be So Mean, Baby." "So, anyway, I went down there," he said. "And there was old Dick. So down, so *blue,* so full of important news that couldn't wait till this afternoon. Sitting at a table in blue jeans and a gruesome sports jacket. The Des Moines expatriate in New York. I could've killed him, I swear to God. What a night. I sat there for two solid hours while he told me what a su*per*ior son of a bitch I am, and what a family of psychotics and psychopathic prodigies I come from. *Then,* when he's all through analyzing me—*and* Bud-

dy, *and* Seymour, both of whom he's never met
—and when he's reached some sort of impasse in
his mind whether he's going to be a sort of two-
fisted Colette or a sort of short Thomas Wolfe
for the rest of the evening, suddenly he pulls out
this gorgeous monogrammed attaché case from
under the table and shoves a new, hour-long
script under my arm." He made a pass at the air
with one hand, as if to dismiss the subject. But
he got up from the piano bench too restively for
it to have been a real gesture of dismissal. His
cigar was in his mouth, his hands were in his hip
pockets. "For *years* I've been listening to Buddy
sound off on the subject of actors," he said. "My
God, what an earful I could give him on the
subject of Writers I've Known." He stood ab-
stracted for a moment, then became aimlessly
mobile. He stopped at the 1920 Victrola, looked
at it blankly, and barked, twice, for his own
amusement, into its megaphone speaker. Franny,
watching him, giggled, but he frowned, and
moved on. At the tropical-fish tank, which was
mounted on top of the 1927 Freshman radio, he
abruptly stooped, taking his cigar out of his
mouth. He peered into the tank with unmis-
takable interest. "All my black mollies are dying
off," he said. He reached, automatically, for the
container of fish food beside the tank.

"Bessie fed them this morning," Franny cau-
tioned him. She was still stroking Bloomberg,
still succoring him, forcibly, into the subtle and
difficult world outside warm afghans.

"They look starved," Zooey said, but withdrew his hand from the fish food. "This guy has a very drawn look." He tapped the glass with his fingernail. "What you need is some chicken soup, buddy."

"Zooey," Franny said, to get his attention. "How does it stand now? You have *two* new scripts. What's the one LeSage dropped by in the cab?"

Zooey went on peering in at the fish for a moment. Then, on a sudden but apparently pressing impulse, he stretched out supine on the carpet. "In the one LeSage sent over," he said, crossing his feet, "I'm supposed to be Rick *Chalm*ers in, I swear to God, a 1928 drawing-room comedy straight out of French's catalogue. The only difference is that it's brought gloriously up to date with a lot of jargon about complexes and repressions and sublimations that the writer brought home from his analyst's."

Franny looked at what she could see of him. Only his soles and heels were visible from where she sat. "Well, what about Dick's thing?" she asked. "Have you read it yet?"

"In Dick's thing, I can be Bernie, a sensitive young subway guard, in the most courageous goddam offbeat television opus you ever read."

"You mean it? Is it really good?"

"I didn't say *good,* I said *courageous.* Let's keep on our toes here, buddy. The morning after it's produced, everybody in the building'll go around slamming each other on the back in an orgy of mutual appreciation. LeSage. Hess. Pomeroy. The sponsors. The whole courageous bunch. It'll all start this afternoon. If it hasn't already. Hess'll go into LeSage's office and say to him, 'Mr. LeSage, sir, I've got a new script about a sensitive young subway guard that just stinks of courage and integrity. And I know, sir, that next to scripts that are Tender and Poignant, you love scripts that have Courage and Integrity. This one, sir, as I say, stinks of both. It's full of melting-pot types. It's sentimental. It's violent in the right places. And just when the sensitive subway guard's problems are getting the best of him, destroying his faith in Mankind and the Little People, his nine-year-old niece comes home from school and gives him some nice, pat chauvinistic philosophy handed down to us through posterity and P.S. 564 all the way from Andrew Jackson's backwoods wife. It can't miss, sir! It's down-to-earth, it's simple, it's untrue, and it's familiar enough and trivial enough to be understood and loved by our greedy, nervous, illiterate sponsors.' " Zooey abruptly raised himself up to a sitting position. "I just took a bath, and I'm sweating like a pig," he commented. He got to his feet, and, doing so, glanced briefly, and as if against his better judgment, at Franny. He started to look away but, instead, looked at her more closely. She had her head down, and her eyes on Bloomberg, in her lap, whom she had continued to stroke. But there was a change. "Ah," Zooey said, and came closer to the couch, apparently looking for trouble. "Madam's lips are moving. The Prayer is rising." Franny didn't look up. "What the hell are you doing?" he asked. "Taking refuge from my un-Christian attitude to the popular arts?"

Franny looked up then, and shook her head, blinking. She smiled at him. Her lips had, in fact, been moving, and were moving now.

"Just don't smile at me, please," Zooey said, evenly, and walked out of the vicinity. "Seymour was always doing that to me. This goddam house is lousy with smilers." At one of the bookcases, he gave a misaligned book an orderly little push with his thumb, then passed on. He went over to the middle window in the room, which was separated by a window seat from the cherry-wood table where Mrs. Glass paid bills and wrote letters. He stood looking out of it, his back to Franny, his hands in his hip pockets again, his cigar in his mouth. "Did you know I may go to France this summer to make a picture?" he asked, irritably. "Did I tell you?"

Franny looked over at his back with interest. "No, you didn't!" she said. "Are you serious? What picture?"

Zooey, looking out over the macadamized school roof across the street, said, "Oh, it's a long story. Some French joker's over here, and he heard the album I did with Philippe. I had lunch with him one day a couple of weeks ago. A real schnorrer, but sort of likable, and apparently he's hot over there right now." He put one foot up on the window seat. "Nothing's final—nothing's ever final with these guys—but I think I've got him half snowed into the idea of making a picture out of that Lenormand novel. The one I sent you."

"Yes! Oh, that's ex*cit*ing, Zooey. If you go, when do you think you'd go?"

"It is *not* exciting. That's exactly the point. I'd enjoy doing it, yes. *God,* yes. But I'd hate like hell to leave New York. If you must know, I hate any kind of so-called creative type who gets on any kind of ship. I don't give a goddam what his reasons are. I was *born* here. I went to *school* here. I've been *run over* here—*twice,* and on the same damn *street.* I have no business acting in Europe, for God's sake."

Franny gazed thoughtfully at his white broadcloth back. Her lips, however, were still silently forming words. "Why do you go, then?" she asked. "If you feel that way."

"Why do I *go?*" Zooey said, without looking around. "I *go* mostly because I'm tired as hell of getting up furious in the morning and going to bed furious at night. I *go* because I sit in judgment on every poor, ulcerous bastard I know. Which in itself doesn't bother me too much. At least, I judge straight from the colon when I judge, and I know that I'll pay like hell for any judgment I mete out, sooner or later, one way or another. *That* doesn't bother me so much. But there's something—Jesus God—there's something I do to people's morale downtown that I can't stand to watch much longer. I can tell you ex*act*ly what I do. I make everybody feel that he doesn't really want to do any good work but that he just wants to get work done that will be thought good by everyone he knows—the critics, the sponsors, the public, even his children's schoolteacher. That's what I do. That's the worst I do." He frowned in the direction of the school roof; then, with his fingertips, pressed some perspiration away from his forehead. He turned, abruptly, toward Franny when he heard her say something. "What?" he said. "I can't hear you."

"Nothing. I said 'Oh, God.' "

"Why 'Oh, God'?" Zooey asked, impatiently.

"Noth-ing. Don't jump on me, please. I was only thinking, that's all. I just wish you could've seen me on Saturday. You talk about undermining people's morale! I absolutely *ruined* Lane's whole day. I not only passed *out* on him every hour on the hour but here I'd gone all the way up there for a nice, friendly, *nor*mal, cocktaily, supposedly *hap*py football game, and absolutely everything he said I either jumped on or contradicted or—I don't know—just spoiled." Franny shook her head. She was still stroking Bloomberg, but absently. The piano appeared to be her focal point. "I simply could *not* keep a single opinion to myself," she said. "It was just horrible. Almost from the very second he met me at the station, I started picking and picking and picking at all his opinions and values and—just everything. But *e*verything. He'd written some perfectly harmless test-tubey paper on Flaubert that he was *so* proud of and wanted me to read, and it just sounded to me so strictly English Department and *p*atronizing and campusy that all I did was—" She broke off. She shook her head again, and Zooey, still half-pivoted in her direction, narrowed his eyes at her. She was looking even paler, more post-operative, as it were, than she had on waking. "It's a wonder he didn't shoot me," she said. "I'd have absolutely con-*grat*ulated him if he had."

"You told me that bit last night. I don't want any unfresh reminiscences this morning, bud-dy," Zooey said, and resumed looking out of the window. "In the first place, you're way off when you start railing at *things* and people instead of at yourself. We both are. I do the same goddam thing about television—I'm aware of that. But it's *wrong*. It's *us*. I keep telling you that. Why are you so damned dense about it?"

"I'm *not* so damned dense about it, but you keep—"

"It's *us*," Zooey repeated, overriding her. "We're freaks, that's all. Those two bastards got us nice and early and made us into freaks with freakish standards, that's all. We're the Tat-tooed Lady, and we're never going to have a minute's peace, the rest of our lives, till every-body else is tattooed, too." More than a trifle grimly, he brought his cigar to his mouth and dragged on it, but it had gone out. "On top of everything else," he said immediately, "we've got 'Wise Child' complexes. We've never really got off the goddam air. Not one of us. We don't talk, we hold forth. We don't converse, we expound. At least *I* do. The minute I'm in a room with somebody who has the usual number of ears, I either turn into a goddam *seer* or a human hatpin. The Prince of Bores. *Last night,* for instance. Down at the San Remo. I kept *pray*ing that Hess wouldn't tell me the plot of his new script. I knew damn well he *had* one. I knew damn well I wasn't going to get out of the place without a new script to take home. But I kept praying he'd spare me from an oral *pre*view. He's not stupid. He *knows* it's impossible for me to keep my mouth shut." Zooey suddenly, sharply, turned around, without taking his foot off the window seat, and picked up, snatched up, a match folder that was on his mother's writing table. He turned back to the window and the view of the school roof and put his cigar into his mouth again—but at once took it out. "*Damn* him, anyway," he said. "He's so stupid it breaks your heart. He's like everybody else in television. *And* Hollywood. *And* Broadway. He thinks everything sentimental is *tender,* everything *brutal* is a slice of *re*alism, and everything that runs into physical violence is a legitimate climax to something that isn't even—"

"Did you *tell* him that?"

"Certainly I told him that! I just got through telling you I can't keep my mouth shut. Certainly I told him that! I left him sitting there wishing he was dead. Or *one* of us was dead— I hope to hell it was me. Anyway, it was a true San Remo exit." Zooey took down his foot from the window seat. He turned around, looking both tense and agitated, and pulled out the straight chair at his mother's writing table and sat down. He relit his cigar, then hunched forward, restively, both arms on the cherrywood surface. An object his mother used as a paperweight stood beside the inkwell: a small glass sphere, on a black plastic pedestal, containing a snowman wearing a stovepipe hat. Zooey picked it up, gave it a shake, and sat apparently watching the snowflakes swirl.

Franny, looking at him, now had a hand visored over her eyes. Zooey was sitting in the main shaft of sunlight in the room. She might have altered her position on the couch, if she meant to go on looking at him, but that would have disturbed Bloomberg, in her lap, who appeared to be asleep. "Do you really have an ulcer?" she asked suddenly. "Mother said you have an ulcer."

"*Yes*, I have an ulcer, for Chrissake. This is Kaliyuga, buddy, the Iron Age. Anybody over sixteen without an ulcer's a goddam spy." He gave the snowman another, more vigorous shake. "The funny part is," he said, "I like Hess. Or at least I like him when he's not shoving his artistic poverty down my throat. At least he wears horrible neckties and funny padded suits in the middle of that frightened, super-conservative, super-conforming madhouse. And I like his conceit. He's so conceited he's actually humble, the crazy bastard. I mean he obviously thinks television's good enough to deserve him and his big, bogus-courageous, 'offbeat' talent—which is a crazy kind of humility, if you feel like thinking about it." He stared at the glass ball till the snowstorm had abated somewhat. "In a way, I sort of like LeSage, too. Everything he owns is the best—his overcoat, his two-cabin cruiser, his son's grades at Harvard, his electric razor, *every*-thing. He took me home to dinner once and stopped me in the driveway to ask me if I remembered 'the late Carole Lombard, in the movies.' He warned me I'd get a shock when I met his wife, she was such a dead ringer for Carole Lombard. I suppose I'll like him for that till I die. His wife turned out to be a really tired, bosomy, Persian-looking blonde." Zooey looked around abruptly at Franny, who had said something. "What?" he asked.

"Yes!" Franny repeated—pale, but beaming, and apparently fated, too, to like Mr. LeSage till death.

Zooey smoked his cigar in silence for a moment. "What gets me so down about Dick Hess," he said, "what makes me so *sad,* or furious, or whatever the hell I am, is that the first script he did for LeSage was pretty good. It was almost *good,* in fact. It was the first one we did on film—I don't think you saw it, you were at

school or something. I played a young farmer
in it who lives all alone with his father. The boy
has a notion that he hates farming, and he and
his father have always had a terrible time making a living, so when the father dies, he sells all
the cattle and makes big plans to go to the big
city to make a living." Zooey picked up the
snowman again but didn't give it a shake—
merely turned it around, by the pedestal. "It
had some nice bits," he said. "After I sell all the
cows, I keep going out to the pasture to look for
them. And when I go for a farewell walk with
my girl, right before I leave for the big city, I
keep steering her over toward the empty pasture.
Then, when I get to the big city and get a job, I
spend all my spare time hanging around the
stockyards. Finally, in heavy traffic on the main
street in the big city, a car makes a left turn and
changes into a cow. I run after it, just as the
light changes, and get run over—stampeded."
He gave the snowman a shake. "It probably
wasn't anything you couldn't watch while you
were cutting your toenails, but at least you
didn't feel like *slinking* home from the studio
after rehearsals. It was fresh enough, at least,
and it was his own, it wasn't part of a hack-
neyed trend in scripts. I wish to hell he'd go
home and fill up again. I wish to hell everybody'd go home. I'm sick to death of being the
heavy in everybody's life. God, you should see
Hess and LeSage when they're talking about a
new show. Or a new *any*thing. They're as happy

as pigs till I show up. I feel like those dismal bastards Seymour's beloved Chuang-tzu warned everybody against. 'Beware when the so-called sagely men come limping into sight.' " He sat still, watching the snowflakes swirl. "I could happily lie down and die sometimes," he said.

Franny at that moment was gazing at a sunlit faded spot in the carpet over near the piano, her lips very discernibly moving. "This is all so funny, you can't imagine," she said, with the faintest tremor in her voice, and Zooey looked over at her. Her paleness was emphasized by the fact that she was wearing no lipstick at all. "Everything you're saying brings back everything I was *try*ing to say to Lane on Saturday, when he started digging at me. Right in the middle of Martinis and snails and things. I mean we're not bothered by exactly the same things, but by the same kind of things, I think, and for the same reasons. At least, it sounds that way." Bloomberg just then stood up in <u>her lap and</u>, more like a dog than a cat, began to circle around to find a sleeping position he liked better. Franny absently, yet like a guide, placed her hands gently on his back, and went on speaking. "I actually reached a point where I said to myself, right out loud, like a lunatic, If I hear just one more picky, *cav*illing, unconstructive word out of you, Franny Glass, you and I are finished—but *fin*-ished. And for a while I wasn't too bad. For about a whole month, at least, whenever anybody said anything that sounded campusy and

phony, or that smelled to high heaven of ego or
something like that, I at least kept quiet about
it. I went to the movies or I stayed in the library
all hours or I started writing papers like mad on
Restoration *Com*edy and stuff like that—but at
least I had the *pleas*ure of not hearing my own
voice for a while." She shook her head. "Then,
one morning—bang, bang, I started up again.
I didn't sleep all night, for some reason, and I
had an eight-o'clock in French Lit, so finally I
just got up and got dressed and made some coffee and then walked around the campus. What
I *wanted* to do was just go for a terribly long
ride on my bike, but I was afraid everybody'd
hear me taking my bike out of the stand—something always *falls*—so I just went to the Lit
building and *sat*. I sat and sat, and finally I got
up and started writing things from Epictetus all
over the blackboard. I filled the whole front
blackboard—I didn't even know I'd remembered so much of him. I erased it—thank God!
—before people started coming in. But it was a
childish thing to do anyway—Epictetus would
have absolutely *hated* me for doing it—but . . ."
Franny hesitated. "I don't know. I think I just
wanted to see the name of somebody *nice* up on
a blackboard. Anyway, that started me up again.
I picked all day. I picked on Professor *Fal*lon. I
picked on *Lane* when I talked to him on the
phone. I picked on Professor *Tup*per. It got
worse and worse. I even started picking on my
roommate. Oh, God, poor Bev! I started catch-

ing her looking at me as if she hoped I'd decide
to move out of the room and let somebody halfway pleasant and *nor*mal move in and give her
a little peace. It was just terrible! And the worst
part was, I *knew* what a bore I was being, I *knew*
how I was depressing people, or even hurting
their *feel*ings—but I just couldn't stop! I just
could not stop picking." Looking more than a
little distrait, she paused just long enough to
push downward on Bloomberg's roving hind-
quarters. "It was the worst of all in class,
though," she said with decision. "That was the
worst. What happened was, I got the idea in my
head—and I could *not* get it out—that college
was just one more *dopey, inane* place in the
world dedicated to piling up treasure on earth
and everything. I mean treasure is *treas*ure, for
heaven's sake. What's the difference whether the
treasure is money, or property, or even *cul*ture,
or even just plain knowledge? It all seemed like
*exact*ly the same thing to me, if you take off the
wrapping—and it still does! Sometimes I think
that *knowl*edge—when it's knowledge for knowledge's sake, anyway—is the worst of all. The
least excusable, certainly." Nervously, and without any real need whatever, Franny pushed back
her hair with one hand. "I don't think it would
have all got me quite so down if just once in a
while—just *once* in a while—there was at least
some polite little per*funct*ory implication that
knowledge *should* lead to *wisdom,* and that if it
doesn't, it's just a disgusting waste of time! But

there never is! You never even hear any *hints* dropped on a campus that wisdom is *supposed* to be the *goal* of knowledge. You hardly ever even hear the word 'wisdom' mentioned! Do you want to hear something funny? Do you want to hear something really funny? In almost four years of college—and this is the absolute *truth* —in almost four years of college, the only time I can remember ever even *hear*ing the expression 'wise man' being used was in my freshman year, in Political Science! And you know how it was used? It was used in reference to some nice old poopy elder statesman who'd made a fortune in the stock market and then gone to Washington to be an adviser to President Roosevelt. *Hon*estly, now! Four years of college, almost! I'm not saying that happens to *ev*erybody, but I just get so *upset* when I think about it I could die." She broke off, and apparently became re-dedicated to serving Bloomberg's interests. Her lips now had very little more color in them than her face. They were also, very faintly, chapped.

Zooey's eyes were on her, and had been. "I want to ask you something, Franny," he said abruptly. He turned back to the writing-table surface again, frowned, and gave the snowman a shake. "What do you think you're doing with the Jesus Prayer?" he asked. "This is what I was trying to get at last night. Before you told me to go chase myself. You talk about piling up treasure—money, property, culture, knowledge, and so on and so on. In going ahead with the Jesus

Prayer—just let me finish, now, please—in going ahead with the Jesus Prayer, aren't you trying to lay up some kind of treasure? Something that's every goddam bit as negotiable as all those other, more material things? Or does the fact that it's a prayer make all the difference? I mean by that, is there all the difference in the world, for you, in which side somebody lays up his treasure—this side, or the other? The one where thieves can't break in, et cetera? Is that what makes the difference? *Wait* a second, now— just wait'll I'm finished, please." He sat for a few seconds watching the little blizzard in the glass sphere. Then: "There's something about the way you're going at this prayer that gives me the *willies,* if you want to know the truth. You think I'm out to stop you from saying it. I don't know whether I am or not—that's a goddam debatable point—but I *would* like you to clear up for me just what the hell your motives are for saying it." He hesitated, but not long enough to give Franny a chance to cut in on him. "As a matter of simple logic, there's no difference at all, that *I* can see, between the man who's greedy for material treasure—or even intellectual treasure—and the man who's greedy for spiritual treasure. As you say, treasure's treasure, God damn it, and it seems to me that ninety per cent of all the world-hating saints in history were just as ac*quis*itive and unattractive, basically, as the rest of us are."

Franny said, as icily as she could with a faint

tremor in her voice, "May I interrupt now, Zooey?"

Zooey let go the snowman and picked up a pencil to play with. "Yes, yes. Interrupt," he said.

"I *know* all you're saying. You're not telling me one thing I haven't thought of by myself. You're saying I *want* something from the Jesus Prayer—which makes me just as acquisitive, in your word, really, as somebody who wants a sable *coat,* or to be *fam*ous, or to be dripping with some kind of crazy pres*tige*. I know all that! My gosh, what kind of an imbecile do you think I am?" The tremor in her voice amounted now almost to an impediment.

"All right, take it easy, take it easy."

"I *can't* take it easy! You make me so mad! What do you think I'm doing here in this crazy room—losing weight like mad, worrying Bessie and Les absolutely silly, upsetting the house, and everything? Don't you think I have sense enough to *worry* about my motives for saying the prayer? That's exactly what's *both*ering me so. Just because I'm choosy about what I want— in this case, en*light*enment, or *peace,* instead of money or pres*tige* or *fame* or any of those things —doesn't mean I'm not as egotistical and self-seeking as everybody else. If anything, I'm more so! I don't need the famous Zachary Glass to tell me that!" Here there was a marked break in her voice, and she began to be very attentive to

Bloomberg again. Tears, presumably, were imminent, if not already on the way.

Over at the writing table, Zooey, pressing down heavily with his pencil, was filling in the "o"s on the advertisement side of a small blotter. He kept this up for a little interval, then flipped the pencil toward the inkwell. He picked up his cigar from the lip of the copper ashtray where he had placed it. It was now only about two inches in length but was still burning. He took a deep drag on it, as if it were a kind of respirator in an otherwise oxygenless world. Then, almost forcibly, he looked over at Franny again. "Do you want me to try to get Buddy on the phone for you tonight?" he asked. "I think you should talk to *some*body—*I'm* no damn good for this." He waited, looking at her steadily. "Franny. What about it?"

Franny's head was bowed. She appeared to be searching for fleas in Bloomberg's coat, her fingers very busy indeed turning back tufts of fur. She was in fact crying now, but in a very local sort of way, as it were; there were tears but no sounds. Zooey watched her for a full minute or so, then said, not precisely kindly, but without importuning, "Franny. What about it? Shall I try to get Buddy on the phone?"

She shook her head, without raising it. She went on searching for fleas. Then, after an interval, she did reply to Zooey's question, but not very audibly.

"What?" Zooey asked.

Franny repeated her statement. "I want to talk to Seymour," she said.

Zooey went on looking at her for a moment, his face essentially expressionless—discounting a line of perspiration on his rather long and singularly Irish upper lip. Then, with characteristic abruptness, he turned back and resumed filling in "o"s. But he put down the pencil almost immediately. He got up from the writing table—rather slowly, for him—and, taking his cigar stub with him, reassumed his one-foot-up stance at the window seat. A taller, longer-legged man—any one of his brothers, for example—might have put his foot up, might have made the stretch, with greater ease. But once Zooey's foot was up, he gave the impression of sustaining a dancer's position.

At first piecemeal, then point-blank, he let his attention be drawn to a little scene that was being acted out sublimely, unhampered by writers and directors and producers, five stories below the window and across the street. A fair-sized maple tree stood in front of the girls' private school—one of four or five trees on that fortunate side of the street—and at the moment a child of seven or eight, female, was hiding behind it. She was wearing a navy-blue reefer and a tam that was very nearly the same shade of red as the blanket on the bed in van Gogh's room at Arles. Her tam did, in fact, from Zooey's vantage point, appear not unlike a dab of paint. Some fifteen feet away from the child, her dog—a young dachshund, wearing a green leather collar and leash—was sniffing to find her, scurrying in frantic circles, his leash dragging behind him. The anguish of separation was scarcely bearable for him, and when at last he picked up his mistress's scent, it wasn't a second too soon. The joy of reunion, for both, was immense. The dachshund gave a little yelp, then cringed forward, shimmying with ecstasy, till his mistress, shouting something at him, stepped hurriedly over the wire guard surrounding the tree and picked him up. She said a number of words of praise to him, in the private argot of the game, then put him down and picked up his leash, and the two walked gaily west, toward Fifth Avenue and the Park and out of Zooey's sight. Zooey reflexively put his hand on a cross-piece between panes of glass, as if he had a mind to raise the window and lean out of it to watch the two disappear. It was his cigar hand, however, and he hesitated a second too long. He dragged on his cigar. "God damn it," he said, "there are nice things in the world—and I mean *nice* things. We're all such morons to get so sidetracked. Always, always, always referring every goddam thing that happens right back to our lousy little egos." Behind him, just then, Franny blew her nose with guileless abandon; the report was considerably louder than might have been expected from so fine and delicate-appearing an organ. Zooey turned around to look at her, somewhat censoriously.

Franny, busy with several folds of Kleenex, looked at him. "Well, I'm *sorry*," she said. "Can't I blow my nose?"

"You finished?"

"*Yes*, I'm finished! My gosh, what a family. You take your life in your hands if you just blow your *nose*."

Zooey turned back to the window. He smoked briefly, his eyes following a pattern of concrete blocks in the school building. "Buddy once said something reasonably sensible to me a couple of years ago," he said. "If I can remember what it was." He hesitated. And Franny, though still busy with her Kleenex, looked over at him. When Zooey appeared to have difficulty in remembering something, his hesitation invariably interested all his brothers and sisters, and even held some entertainment value for them. His hesitations were almost always specious. Most of the time, they were direct carry-overs from the five undoubtedly formative years he had spent as a regular panelist on "It's a Wise Child," when, rather than seem to flaunt his somewhat preposterous ability to quote, instantaneously and, usually, verbatim, almost anything he had ever read, or even listened to, with genuine interest, he cultivated a habit of furrowing his brow and appearing to stall for time, the way the other children on the program did. His brow was furrowed now, but he spoke up rather more quickly than was customary under the circumstances, as though he sensed that Franny, his old co-panelist, had caught him at it. "He said that a man should be able to lie at the bottom of a hill with his throat cut, slowly bleeding to death, and if a pretty girl or an old woman should pass by with a beautiful jug balanced perfectly on the top of her head, he should be able to raise himself up on one arm and see the jug safely over the top of the hill." He thought this over, then gave a mild snort. "I'd like to see him do it, the bastard." He took a drag on his cigar. "Everybody in this family gets his goddam religion in a different package," he commented, with a notable absence of awe in his tone. "Walt was a hot one. Walt and Boo Boo had the hottest religious philosophies in the family." He dragged on his cigar, as if to offset being amused when he didn't care to be. "Walt once told Waker that everybody in the family must have piled up one *helluva* lot of bad karma in his past incarnations. He had a theory, Walt, that the religious life, and all the agony that goes with it, is just something God sicks on people who have the gall to accuse Him of having created an ugly world."

A titter of audience appreciation came from the couch. "I never heard that," Franny said. "What's Boo Boo's religious philosophy? I didn't think she had any."

Zooey said nothing for a moment, and then: "Boo Boo's? Boo Boo's convinced Mr. Ashe made the world. She got it from Kilvert's 'Diary.' The schoolchildren in Kilvert's parish were asked who made the world, and one of the kids answered, 'Mr. Ashe.' "

Franny was delighted, and audibly so. Zooey turned and looked at her, and—unpredictable young man—made a very dour face, as though he had suddenly eschewed any and all forms of levity. He took down his foot from the window seat, parked his cigar end in the copper ashtray on the writing table, and came away from the window. He moved across the room slowly, hands in his hip pockets, but not without some direction in his mind. "I should get the hell out of here. I've got a lunch date," he said, and immediately stooped to make a leisurely and proprietary examination of the interior of the fish tank. He tapped on the glass with his fingernail, importunately. "I turn my back for five minutes and everybody lets my black mollies die off. I should've taken them to college with me. I *knew* that."

"Oh, Zooey. You've been saying that for five years. Why don't you go buy some new ones?"

He went on tapping on the glass. "All you college snips are the same. Hard as nails. These weren't just any black mollies, buddy. We were very close." So saying, he stretched out on his back on the carpet again, his slight torso fitting in rather tightly between the 1932 Stromberg-Carlson table radio and an overfilled maple magazine stand. Again only the soles and heels of his brogues were visible to Franny. However, no sooner was he stretched out than he sat bolt

upright, his head and shoulders suddenly pro-
pelled into view, with somewhat the macabre-
comic effect of a corpse falling out of a closet.
"Prayer's still going, eh?" he said. Then he
dropped back out of sight again. He was still for
a moment. Then, in an almost unintelligibly
thick Mayfair accent: "I'd rather like a word
with you, Miss Glass, if you've a moment." The
response to this, over at the couch, was a distinctly ominous silence. "Say your prayer if you
want to, or play with Bloomberg, or feel free to
smoke, but give me five minutes of uninter-
rupted silence, buddy. And, if possible, *no tears
at all.* O.K.? You hear me?"

Franny didn't answer straightway. She brought
her legs in closer to her, under the afghan. And
gathered in the sleeping Bloomberg somewhat
closer to her, too. "I hear you," she said, and
drew her legs in still closer to her, as a fortress
draws up its bridge before the siege. She hesitated, then spoke up again. "You can say anything you want if you don't get abusive about it.
I just don't feel like a workout this morning.
I mean it."

"No workouts, no workouts, buddy. And if
there's one thing I never am, it's abusive." The
speaker's hands were folded benignly on his
chest. "Oh, a little *brisk* sometimes, yes, when
the situation warrants. Abusive, never. Personally, I've always found that you can catch more
flies with—"

"I *mean* it, now, Zooey," Franny said, more

or less addressing his brogues. "And I wish you'd sit up, incidentally. Every time all hell breaks loose around here, it seems very *funny* to me that it always comes from that spot right where you're lying. And you're always the one that's there. C'mon, now. Just please sit up."

Zooey closed his eyes. "Fortunately, I know you don't mean that. Not deep down. We both know, deep in our hearts, that this is the only piece of hallowed ground in this whole goddam haunted house. This *hap*pens to be where I used to keep my rabbits. And they were *saints,* both of them. As a matter of fact, they were the only celibate rabbits in the—"

"Oh, shut up!" Franny said, nervously. "Just *start,* if you're going to. All I ask is that you at least try to be a little bit *tact*ful, the way I'm feeling right now—that's all. You are without a doubt the most tactless person I've ever known in my life."

"Tactless! *Never.* Outspoken, yes. High-spirited, yes. *Met*tlesome. *San*guine, perhaps, to a fault. But no one has ever—"

"I said *tact*less!" Franny overrode him. With considerable heat, yet trying not to be amused. "Just get sick sometime and go visit yourself, and you'll find out how tactless you are! You're the most impossible person to have around when somebody's not feeling up to par that I've ever known in my *life.* If somebody just has a *cold,* even, you know what you do? You give them a dirty look every time you see them. You're absolutely the most unsympa*thet*ic person I've ever known. You are!"

"All right, all right, all right," Zooey said, with his eyes still closed. "Nobody's perfect, buddy." Effortlessly, by softening and thinning his voice, rather than by raising it to a falsetto, he gave what was to Franny a familiar and always realistic imitation of their mother passing along a few cautionary words: "We say many things in *heat*, young lady, that we don't really *mean* and are very *sorry* for the next day." Then, instantly, he frowned, opened his eyes, and stared for several seconds at the ceiling. "Firstly," he said, "I think you think I have intentions of trying to take your prayer away from you or something. I don't. I do not. You can lie on that couch reciting the preamble to the Cons*tit*ution for the rest of your life, as far as I'm concerned, but what I *am* trying—"

"That's a beautiful start. Just *beaut*iful."

"Beg pardon?"

"Oh, shut up. Just go on, go *on*."

"What I started to say, I have nothing against the prayer at all. No matter what you think. You're not the *first* one who ever thought of saying it, you know. I once went to every Army & Navy store in New York looking for a nice, pilgrim-type rucksack. I was going to fill it with bread crumbs and start walking all over the goddam country. Saying the prayer. Spreading the Word. The whole business." Zooey hesitated. "And I don't just mention it, for God's sake, to show you I was once an Emotional Young Person Just Like Yourself."

"Why *do* you mention it, then?"

"Why do I mention it? I mention it because I have a couple of things I want to say to you, and it's just possible I'm not qualified to say them. On the ground that I once had a strong desire to say the prayer myself but didn't. For all I know, I may be a little jealous of your having a go at it. It's very possible, in fact. In the first place, I'm a ham. It may very well be that I hate like hell to play Martha to somebody else's Mary. Who the hell knows?"

Franny didn't choose to reply. But she drew Bloomberg slightly closer to her and gave him an odd, ambiguous little hug. Then she looked over in her brother's direction, and said, "You're a brownie. Did you know that?"

"Just hold the compliments, buddy—you may live to retract them. I'm still going to tell you what I don't like about the way you're going at this business. Qualified or not." Here Zooey stared blankly at the plaster ceiling for a matter of ten seconds or so, then closed his eyes again. "Firstly," he said, "I don't like this Camille routine. And don't interrupt me, now. I know you're legitimately falling apart, and all that. And I don't think it's an *act*—I don't mean that. And I don't think it's a subconscious plea for *symp*athy. Or any of that business. But I still say I don't like it. It's rough on *Bessie,* it's rough on *Les*—and if you don't know it yet, you're beginning to give off a little stink of piousness. God damn it, there isn't any prayer in any religion in the world that justifies piousness. I'm not saying you *are* pious—so just sit still—but I *am* saying all this hysteria business is unattractive as *hell*."

"Are you finished?" Franny said, sitting very notably forward. The tremor had returned to her voice.

"All right, Franny. C'mon, now. You said you'd hear me out. I've said the worst, I think. I'm just trying to tell you—I'm not *try*ing, I'm telling you—that this just is not fair to Bessie and Les. It's *terrible* for them—and you know it. Did you know, God damn it, that Les was all for bringing a tanger*ine* in to you last night before he went to bed? My God. Even Bessie can't stand stories with tangerines in them. And God knows *I* can't. If you're going to go on with this breakdown business, I wish to hell you'd go back to college to have it. Where you're not the baby of the family. And where, God knows, nobody'll have any urges to bring you any tangerines. And where you don't keep your goddam *tap* shoes in the closet."

Franny, at this point, reached rather blindly, but soundlessly, for the box of Kleenex on the marble coffee table.

Zooey was now gazing abstractedly at an old root-beer stain on the ceiling plaster, which he himself had made nineteen or twenty years earlier, with a water pistol. "The next thing that bothers me," he said, "isn't pretty, either. But I'm almost finished, so hang on a second if you can. What I don't like at *all* is this little hair-shirty private life of a martyr you're living back at college—this little snotty crusade you think you're leading against everybody. And I don't mean what you may think I mean, so try not to interrupt for a second. I take it that mostly you're gunning against the system of higher education. Don't *spring* at me, now—for the most part, I agree with you. But I hate the kind of blanket attack you're making on it. I agree with you about ninety-eight per cent on the issue. But the other two per cent scares me half to death. I had one professor when I was in college—just *one,* I'll grant you, but he was a big, big one—who just doesn't fit in with anything you've been talking about. He wasn't Epic*tet*us. But he was no egomaniac, he was no faculty charm boy. He was a great and modest scholar. And what's more, I don't think I ever heard him say anything, either in or out of a classroom, that didn't seem to me to have a little bit of real wisdom in it—and sometimes a lot of it. What'll happen to *him* when you start your revolution? I can't bear to think about it—let's change the goddam subject. These other people you've been ranting about are something else again. This Professor Tupper. And those other two goons you were telling me about last night —Manlius, and the other one. I've had *them* by the dozens, and so has everybody else, and I

agree they're not harmless. They're lethal as
hell, as a matter of fact. God almighty. They
make everything they touch turn absolutely academic and useless. Or—worse—*cultish.* To my
mind, they're mostly to blame for the mob of
ignorant oafs with diplomas that are turned
loose on the country every June." Here Zooey,
still looking at the ceiling, simultaneously grimaced and shook his head. "But what I don't like
—and what I don't think either Seymour or
Buddy would like, *either,* as a matter of fact—
is the way you talk about all these people. I
mean you don't just despise what they represent
—you despise *them.* It's too damn personal,
Franny. I mean it. You get a real little homi-
cidal glint in your eye when you talk about this
Tupper, for instance. All this business about his
going into the men's room to muss his hair before he comes in to class. All that. He probably
does—it goes with everything else you've told
me about him. I'm not saying it doesn't. But it's
none of your business, buddy, what he does with
his hair. It would be all right, in a way, if you
thought his personal affectations were sort of
funny. Or if you felt a tiny bit sorry for him for
being insecure enough to give himself a little
pathetic goddam glamour. But when *you* tell
me about it—and I'm not fooling, now—you
tell me about it as though his hair was a goddam
personal enemy of yours. That is *not right*—and
you know it. If you're going to go to war against
the System, just do your shooting like a nice,

intelligent girl—because the enemy's *there,* and not because you don't like his hairdo or his goddam necktie."

A silence followed for a minute or so. It was broken only by the sound of Franny blowing her nose—an abandoned, protracted, "congested" blow, suggestive of a patient with a four-day-old head cold.

"It's exactly like this damned ulcer I picked up. Do you know why I have it? Or at least nine-tenths of the reason I have it? Because when I'm not thinking properly, I let my feelings about television and everything else get personal. I do exactly the same thing you do, and I'm old enough to know better." Zooey paused. His gaze fixed on the root-beer spot, he took a deep breath, through his nose. His fingers were still laced across his chest. "This last thing," he said abruptly, "will probably cause an explosion. But I can't help it. It's the most important thing of all." He appeared to consult the ceiling plaster briefly, then closed his eyes. "I don't know if you remember, but I remember a time around here, buddy, when you were going through a little apostasy from the New Testament that could be heard for miles around. Everybody was in the goddam Army at the time, and I was the one that got his ear bent. But do you remember? Do you remember it at all?"

"I was all of ten years old!" Franny said—nasally, rather dangerously.

"I know how old you were. I know very well

how old you were. C'mon, now. I'm not bringing this up with the idea of throwing anything
back in your teeth—my *God*. I'm bringing this
up for a good reason. I'm bringing it up because
I don't think you understood Jesus when you
were a child and I don't think you understand
him now. I think you've got him confused in
your mind with about five or ten other religious
personages, and I *don't* see how you can go
ahead with the Jesus Prayer till you know who's
who and what's what. Do you remember at all
what started off that little apostasy? . . . Franny?
Do you remember, or don't you?"

He didn't get an answer. Only the sound of a
nose being rather violently blown.

"Well, I do, it happens. Matthew, Chapter
Six. I remember it very clearly, buddy. I even
remember where I *was*. I was back in my room
putting some friction tape on my goddam hockey
stick, and you banged in—all in an uproar, with
the Bible wide open. You didn't like Jesus any
more, and you wanted to know if you could call
Seymour at his Army camp and tell him all
about it. And you know why you didn't like
Jesus any more? I'll tell you. Because, *one,* you
didn't approve of his going into the synagogue
and throwing all the tables and idols all over the
place. That was very rude, very Unnecessary.
You were sure that Solomon or somebody
wouldn't have done anything like that. And the
other thing you disapproved of—the thing you
had the Bible open to—was the lines 'Behold

the fowls of the air: for they sow not, neither do they reap, nor gather into barns; yet your heavenly Father feedeth them.' *That* was all right. That was lovely. That you approved of. *But*, when Jesus says in the same breath, 'Are ye not much better than they?'—*ah*, that's where little Franny gets off. That's where little Franny quits the Bible cold and goes straight to Buddha, who doesn't discriminate against all those nice fowls of the air. All those sweet, lovely chickens and geese that we used to keep up at the Lake. And don't tell me again that you were ten years old. Your age has nothing to do with what I'm talking about. There are no big *changes* between ten and twenty—or ten and eighty, for that matter. You *still* can't love a Jesus as much as you'd like to who did and said a couple of things he was at least reported to have said or done—and you know it. You're constitutionally unable to love or under*stand* any son of God who throws tables around. And you're constitutionally unable to love or understand any son of God who says a human being, *any* human being—even a Professor Tupper—is more valuable to God than any soft, helpless Easter chick."

Franny was now facing directly into the sound of Zooey's voice, sitting bolt upright, a wad of Kleenex clenched in one hand. Bloomberg was no longer in her lap. "I suppose *you can*," she said, shrilling.

"It's beside the point whether *I* can or not. But, yes, as a matter of fact, I can. I don't feel

like going into it, but at least I've never tried,
consciously or otherwise, to turn Jesus into St.
Francis of Assisi to make him more 'lovable'—
which is exactly what ninety-eight per cent of
the Christian world has always insisted on doing.
Not that it's to my credit. I don't happen to be
attracted to the St. Francis of Assisi type. But
you are. And, in my opinion, that's one of the
reasons why you're having this little nervous
breakdown. And es*pec*ially the reason why
you're having it at home. This place is made to
order for you. The service is good, and there's
plenty of hot and cold running ghosts. What
could be more convenient? You can say your
prayer here and roll Jesus and St. Francis and
Seymour and Heidi's grandfather all in one."
Zooey's voice stopped, very briefly. "Can't you
see that? Can't you *see* how unclearly, how slop-
pily, you're looking at things? My God, there's
absolutely nothing tenth-rate about you, and yet
you're up to your neck at this minute in tenth-
rate thinking. Not only is the way you're going
at your prayer tenth-rate re*lig*ion but, whether
you know it or not, you're having a tenth-rate
nervous breakdown. I've seen a couple of real
breakdowns, and the people who had them
didn't bother to pick and choose the place
they—"

"Just stop it, Zooey! Just *stop* it!" Franny
said, sobbing.

"I will, in a minute, in just a minute. Why
are you breaking down, incidentally? I mean if

you're able to go into a collapse with all your might, why can't you use the same energy to stay well and busy? All right, so I'm being unreasonable. I'm being very unreasonable now. But, my God, how you try what little patience I was born with! You take a look around your college *camp*us, and the *world,* and *pol*itics, and one season of summer *stock,* and you listen to the conversation of a bunch of nitwit college students, and you decide that everything's ego, ego, ego, and the only intelligent thing for a girl to do is to lie around and shave her head and say the Jesus Prayer and beg God for a little mystical experience that'll make her nice and happy."

Franny shrieked, *"Will you shut up, please?"*

"In just a second, in just a second. You keep talking about *ego.* My God, it would take Christ himself to decide what's ego and what isn't. This is *God's* universe, buddy, not yours, and he has the final say about what's ego and what isn't. What about your beloved Epictetus? Or your beloved Emily *Dick*inson? You want your Emily, every time she has an urge to write a poem, to just sit down and say a prayer till her nasty, egotistical urge goes away? *No,* of course you don't! But you'd like your friend Professor Tupper's ego taken away from him. That's different. And maybe it is. Maybe it is. But don't go screaming about egos in general. In my opinion, if you really want to know, half the nastiness in the world is stirred up by people who aren't using their true egos. Take your Professor Tupper. From what you say about him, anyway, I'd lay almost any odds that this thing he's using, the thing you think is his ego, isn't his ego at all but some other, much dirtier, much less *basic* faculty. My God, you've been around schools long enough to know the score. Scratch an incompetent schoolteacher—or, for that matter, college professor—and half the time you find a displaced first-class automobile mechanic or a goddam *stone*mason. Take LeSage, for instance— my friend, my employer, my Rose of Madison Avenue. You think it was his ego that got him into television? Like hell it was! He *has* no ego any more—if ever he had one. He's split it up into *hob*bies. He has at least three hobbies that I know of—and they all have to do with a big, ten-thousand-dollar workroom in his basement, full of power tools and vises and God knows what else. Nobody who's really using his ego, his real ego, has any *time* for any goddam hobbies." Zooey suddenly broke off. He was still lying with his eyes closed and his fingers laced, quite tightly, across his chest, his shirt-front. But he now ground his face into a deliberately pained expression—a form, apparently, of self-criticism. "*Hob*bies," he said. "How did I get off onto *hob*bies?" He lay still for a moment.

Franny's sobs, no more than partly muffled by a satin pillow, made the only sound in the room. Bloomberg was now sitting under the piano, on

an island of sunshine, rather picturesquely wash-
ing his face.

"Always the heavy," Zooey said, a trifle too
matter-of-factly. "No matter what I say, I sound
as though I'm undermining your Jesus Prayer.
And I'm *not,* God damn it. All I *am* is against
why and how and *where* you're using it. I'd like
to be convinced—I'd *love* to be convinced—
that you're not using it as a substitute for doing
whatever the hell your duty is in life, or just
your daily duty. Worse than that, though, I can't
see—I swear to God I can't—how you can pray
to a Jesus you don't even understand. And
what's really inexcusable, considering that you've
been funnel-*fed* on just about the same amount
of religious phi*los*ophy that I have—what's really
inexcusable is that you don't try to understand
him. There'd be some excuse for it if you were
either a very *simple* person, like the pilgrim, or
a very goddam *des*perate person—but you're
not simple, buddy, and you're not that damned
desperate." Just then, for the first time since he
had lain down, Zooey, with his eyes still shut,
compressed his lips—very much, as a matter of
parenthetical fact, in the habitual style of his
mother. "God almighty, Franny," he said. "If
you're going to say the Jesus Prayer, at least say
it to *Je*sus, and not to St. Francis and Seymour
and Heidi's grandfather all wrapped up in one.
Keep *him* in mind if you say it, and him only,
and him as he was and not as you'd like him to
have been. You don't face any facts. This same

damned attitude of not facing facts is what got you into this messy state of mind in the first place, and it can't possibly get you out of it."

Zooey abruptly placed his hands over his now quite damp face, left them there for an instant, then removed them. He refolded them. His voice picked up again, almost perfectly conversational in tone. "The part that stumps me, really stumps me, is that I can't see why anybody—unless he was a child, or an angel, or a lucky simpleton like the pilgrim—would even want to say the prayer to a Jesus who was the least bit different from the way he looks and sounds in the New Testament. My God! He's only the most intelligent man in the Bible, that's all! Who isn't he head and shoulders over? *Who?* Both Testaments are full of pundits, prophets, disciples, favorite *sons,* Solomons, Isaiahs, Davids, Pauls —but, my God, who besides Jesus really knew which end was up? *Nobody.* Not Moses. Don't tell me Moses. He was a nice man, and he kept in beautiful touch with his God, and all that— but that's exactly the point. He had to keep in touch. Jesus realized there *is* no separation from God." Zooey here clapped his hands together— only once, and not loud, and very probably in spite of himself. His hands were refolded across his chest almost, as it were, before the clap was out. "Oh, my God, what a mind!" he said. "Who else, for example, would have kept his mouth shut when Pilate asked for an explanation? Not Solomon. Don't say Solomon. Solo-

mon would have had a few pithy words for the
occasion. I'm not sure *Soc*rates wouldn't have,
for that matter. Crito, or somebody, would have
managed to pull him aside just long enough to
get a couple of well-chosen words for the record.
But most of all, above everything else, who in
the Bible besides Jesus knew—*knew*—that we're
carrying the Kingdom of Heaven around with
us, *inside,* where we're all too goddam stupid
and sentimental and unimaginative to look? You
have to *be* a son of God to know that kind of
stuff. Why don't you think of these things? I
mean it, Franny, I'm being serious. When you
don't see Jesus for exactly what he was, you miss
the whole point of the Jesus Prayer. If you don't
understand Jesus, you can't understand his
prayer—you don't get the prayer at all, you just
get some kind of organized cant. Jesus was a
supreme *adept,* by God, on a terribly important
mission. This was no St. Francis, with enough
time to knock out a few canticles, or to preach
to the *birds,* or to do any of the other endearing
things so close to Franny Glass's heart. I'm being
serious now, God damn it. How can you miss
seeing that? If God had wanted somebody with
St. Francis's consistently winning personality for
the job in the New Testament, he'd've picked
him, you can be sure. As it was, he picked the
best, the smartest, the most loving, the least sentimental, the most un*im*itative master he could
possibly have picked. And when you miss seeing
that, I swear to you, you're missing the whole

point of the Jesus Prayer. The Jesus Prayer has one aim, and one aim *only*. To endow the person who says it with Christ-Consciousness. *Not* to set up some little cozy, holier-than-thou trysting place with some sticky, adorable divine *per*sonage who'll take you in his arms and relieve you of all your duties and make all your nasty *Weltschmerzen* and Professor Tuppers go away and never come back. And by God, if you have intelligence enough to see that—and you *do*—and yet you refuse to see it, then you're misusing the prayer, you're using it to ask for a world full of dolls and saints and no Professor Tuppers." He suddenly sat up, shot forward, with an almost calisthenic-like swiftness, to look at Franny. His shirt was, in the familiar phrase, wringing wet. "If Jesus had intended the prayer to be used for—"

Zooey broke off. He stared over at Franny's prostrate, face-down position on the couch, and heard, probably for the first time, the only partly stifled sounds of anguish coming from her. In an instant, he turned pale—pale with anxiety for Franny's condition, and pale, presumably, because failure had suddenly filled the room with its invariably sickening smell. The color of his pallor, however, was a curiously basic white —unmixed, that is, with the greens and yellows of guilt or abject contrition. It was very like the standard bloodlessness in the face of a small boy who loves animals to distraction, *all* animals, and who has just seen his favorite, bunny-loving sister's expression as she opened the box containing his birthday present to her—a freshly caught young cobra, with a red ribbon tied in an awkward bow around its neck.

He stared at Franny for a full minute, then got to his feet, with a little, uncharacteristically awkward movement of imbalance. He went, very slowly, over to his mother's writing table, on the other side of the room. And it was clear, on arrival, that he had no idea why he'd gone over to it. He seemed unfamiliar with the things on the table surface—the blotter with his filled-in "o"s, the ashtray with his cigar end in it—and he turned around and looked at Franny again. Her sobbing had let up a bit, or seemed to have, but her body was in the same wretched, prostrate, face-down position. One arm was bent under her, caught under her, in a way that must have been acutely uncomfortable, if not rather painful. Zooey looked away from her, and then, not unbravely, back at her. He wiped his brow briefly with the palm of his hand, put the hand into his hip pocket to dry it, and said, "I'm sorry, Franny. I'm very sorry." But this formal apology only reactivated, reamplified, Franny's sobbing. He looked at her, fixedly, for another fifteen or twenty seconds. Then he left the room, via the hall, closing the doors behind him.

THE fresh-paint smell was now quite strong just outside the living room. The hall itself had not yet been painted, but newspapers had been strewn the entire length of the hardwood floor, and Zooey's first step—an indecisive, almost dazed one—left the imprint of his rubber heel on a sports-section photograph of Stan Musial holding up a fourteen-inch brook trout. On his fifth or sixth step, he barely missed colliding with his mother, who had just come out of her bedroom. "I thought you'd gone!" she said. She was carrying two laundered and folded cotton bedspreads. "I thought I heard the front—" She broke off to take in Zooey's general appearance. "What *is* that? Prespiration?" she asked. Without waiting for a reply, she took Zooey by the arm and led him—almost swept him, as if he were as light as a broom—into the daylight coming out of her freshly painted bedroom. "It *is* prespiration." Her tone couldn't have held more wonder and censure if Zooey's pores had been exuding crude oil. "What in the world have you been doing? You just had a *bath*. What have you been *do*ing?"

"I'm late now, Fatty. C'mon. One side," Zooey said. A Philadelphia highboy had been moved out into the hall, and, together with Mrs. Glass's person, it blocked Zooey's passage. "Who put this monstrosity out here?" he said, glancing at it.

"Why are you perspiring like that?" Mrs. Glass demanded, staring first at the shirt, then at him. "Did you talk to Franny? Where've you just been? The living room?"

"Yes, *yes*, the living room. And if I were you,

incidentally, I'd go look in there for a second. She's crying. Or was when I left." He tapped his mother on the shoulder. "C'mon, now. I mean it. Get out of the—"

"She's crying? Again? Why? What happened?"

"*I* don't know, for Chrissake—I hid her Pooh books. Come *on*, Bessie, step aside, please. I'm in a hurry."

Mrs. Glass, still staring at him, let him pass. Then, almost at once, she made for the living room, at a clip that scarcely gave her leave to call back over her shoulder, "Change that shirt, young man!"

If Zooey heard this, he gave no sign. At the far end of the hall, he went into the bedroom he had once shared with his twin brothers, which now, in 1955, was his alone. But he stayed in his room for not more than two minutes. When he came out, he had on the same sweaty shirt. There was, however, a slight but fairly distinct change in his appearance. He had acquired a cigar, and lighted it. And for some reason he had an unfolded white handkerchief draped over his head, possibly to ward off rain, or hail, or brimstone.

He went directly across the hall and into the room his two eldest brothers had shared.

This was the first time in almost seven years that Zooey had, in the ready-made dramatic idiom, "set foot" in Seymour's and Buddy's old room. Discounting a totally negligible incident a couple of years earlier, when he had methodi-

cally dragged the entire apartment for a mislaid
or "stolen" tennis-racket press.

He closed the door behind him as tightly as
possible, and with an expression implying that
the absence of a key in the lock met with his
disapproval. He gave the room itself scarcely a
glance, once he was inside it. Instead, he turned
around and deliberately faced a sheet of what
had once been snow-white beaverboard that was
nailed uncompromisingly to the back of the
door. It was a mammoth specimen, very nearly
as long and as wide as the door itself. One could
have believed that its whiteness, smoothness,
and expanse had at one time cried out rather
plaintively for India ink and block lettering.
Certainly not in vain, if so. Every inch of visible surface of the board had been decorated,
with four somewhat gorgeous-looking columns
of quotations from a variety of the world's liter-
atures. The lettering was minute, but jet-black
and passionately legible, if just a trifle fancy in
spots, and without blots or erasures. The work-
manship was no less fastidious even at the bottom of the board, near the doorsill, where the
two penmen, each in his turn, had obviously
lain on their stomachs. No attempt whatever
had been made to assign quotations or authors
to categories or groups of any kind. So that to
read the quotations from top to bottom, column
by column, was rather like walking through an
emergency station set up in a flood area, where,
for example, Pascal had been unribaldly bedded

down with Emily Dickinson, and where, so to speak, Baudelaire's and Thomas à Kempis's toothbrushes were hanging side by side.

Zooey, standing in just close enough, read the top entry in the left-hand column, then went on reading downward. From his expression, or lack of it, he might have been killing time on a railway platform reading a billboard advertisement for Dr. Scholl's foot pads.

You have the right to work, but for the work's sake only. You have no right to the fruits of work. Desire for the fruits of work must never be your motive in working. Never give way to laziness, either.

Perform every action with your heart fixed on the Supreme Lord. Renounce attachment to the fruits. Be even-tempered [underlined by one of the calligraphers] in success and failure; for it is this evenness of temper which is meant by yoga.

Work done with anxiety about results is far inferior to work done without such anxiety, in the calm of self-surrender. Seek refuge in the knowledge of Brahman. They who work selfishly for results are miserable.　　　　　　　—"Bhagavad Gita."

It loved to happen.　　　　　　—Marcus Aurelius.

　　O snail
Climb Mount Fuji,
　　But slowly, slowly!　　　　　　—Issa.

Concerning the Gods, there are those who deny the very existence of the Godhead; others say that it exists, but neither bestirs nor concerns itself nor has forethought for anything. A third party attribute to it existence and forethought, but only for great and heavenly matters, not for anything that is on earth. A fourth party admit things on earth as well as in heaven, but only in general, and not with respect to each individual. A fifth, of whom were Ulysses and Socrates, are those that cry: —

"I move not without Thy knowledge!"

—Epictetus.

The love interest and climax would come when a man and a lady, both strangers, got to talking together on the train going back east.

"Well," said Mrs. Croot, for it was she, "what did you think of the Canyon?"

"Some cave," replied her escort.

"What a funny way to put it!" replied Mrs. Croot. "And now play me something."

—Ring Lardner ("How to Write Short Stories").

God instructs the heart, not by ideas but by pains and contradictions.　　　　　—De Caussade.

"Papa!" shrieked Kitty, and shut his mouth with her hands.

"Well, I won't . . ." he said. "I'm very, very pleased. . . . Oh, what a fool I am. . . ."

He embraced Kitty, kissed her face, her hand, her face again, and made the sign of the cross over her.

And there came over Levin a new feeling of love for this man, till then so little known to him, when he saw how slowly and tenderly Kitty kissed his muscular hand.　　　　　—"Anna Karenina."

"Sir, we ought to teach the people that they are doing wrong in worshipping the images and pictures in the temple."

Ramakrishna: "That's the way with you Calcutta people: you want to teach and preach. You want to give millions when you are beggars yourselves. . . . Do you think God does not know that he is being worshipped in the images and pictures? If a worshipper should make a mistake, do you not think God will know his intent?"

—"The Gospel of Sri Ramakrishna."

"Don't you want to join us?" I was recently asked by an acquaintance when he ran across me alone after midnight in a coffeehouse that was already almost deserted. "No, I don't," I said. —Kafka.

The happiness of being with people. —Kakfa.

St. Francis de Sales' prayer: "Yes, Father! Yes, and always, Yes!"

Zui-Gan called out to himself every day, "Master."

Then he answered himself, "Yes, sir."

And then he added, "Become sober."

Again he answered, "Yes, sir."

"And after that," he continued, "do not be deceived by others."

"Yes, sir; yes, sir," he replied. —Mu-Mon-Kwan.

The lettering on the beaverboard being as small as it was, this last entry appeared well in the upper fifth of its column, and Zooey could have gone on reading for another five minutes or so, staying in the same column, without having to bend his knees. He didn't choose to. He turned around, not abruptly, and walked over and sat down at his brother Seymour's desk—pulling out the little straight chair as though it were something he did every day. He placed his cigar on the right-hand edge of the desk, burning end out, leaned forward on his elbows, and covered his face with his hands.

Behind him and at his left, two curtained windows, with their blinds half drawn, faced into a court—an unpicturesque brick-and-concrete valley through which cleaning women and grocery boys passed grayly at all hours of the day. The room itself was what might be called the third master bedroom of the apartment, and was, by more or less traditional Manhattan apartment-house standards, both unsunny and unlarge. The two eldest Glass boys, Seymour and Buddy, had moved into it in 1929, at the respective ages of twelve and ten, and had vacated it when they were twenty-three and twenty-one. Most of the furniture belonged to a maplewood "set": two day beds, a night table, two boyishly small, knee-cramping desks, two chiffoniers, two semi-easy chairs. Three domestic Oriental scatter rugs, extremely worn, were on the floor. The rest, with very little exaggeration, was books. Meant-to-be-picked-up books. Permanently-left-behind books. Uncertain-what-to-do-with books. But books, books. Tall cases lined three walls of the room, filled to and beyond capacity. The overflow had been piled in stacks on the floor. There was little space left for walking, and none whatever for pacing. A stranger with a flair for cocktail-party descriptive prose might have commented that the room, at a quick glance, looked as if it had once been tenanted by two struggling twelve-year-old lawyers or researchists. And, in fact, unless one chose to make a fairly thoughtful survey of the reading matter extant, there were few, if any, certain indications that the former occupants had both reached voting age within the predominantly juvenile dimensions of the room. True, there was a phone—the controversial private phone—on Buddy's desk. And there were a number of cigarette burns on both desks. But other, more emphatic signs of adulthood— stud or cuff-button boxes, wall pictures, the telling odds and ends that collect on chiffonier tops —had been removed from the room in 1940, when the two young men "branched out" and took an apartment of their own.

With his face in his hands and his handkerchief headgear drooping low over his brow, Zooey sat at Seymour's old desk, inert, but not asleep, for a good twenty minutes. Then, almost in one movement, he removed the support for his face, picked up his cigar, stowed it in his mouth, opened the left-hand bottom drawer of the desk, and took out, using both hands, a seven- or eight-inch-thick stack of what appeared to be—and were—shirt cardboards. He placed the stack before him on the desk and began to turn the cards over, two or three at a time. His hand stayed only once, really, and then quite briefly.

The cardboard that he stopped at had been written on in February, 1938. The handwriting, in blue-lead pencil, was his brother Seymour's:

My twenty-first birthday. Presents, presents, presents. Zooey and the baby, as usual, shopped lower Broadway. They gave me a fine supply of itching powder and a box of three stink bombs. I'm to drop the bombs in the elevator at Columbia or "someplace very crowded" as soon as I get a good chance.

Several acts of vaudeville tonight for my entertainment. Les and Bessie did a lovely soft-shoe on sand swiped by Boo Boo from the urn in the lobby. When they were finished, B. and Boo Boo did a pretty funny imitation of them. Les nearly in tears. The baby sang "Abdul Abulbul Amir." Z. did the Will Mahoney exit Les taught him, ran smack into the bookcase, and was *furious*. The twins did B.'s and my old Buck & Bubbles imitation. But to perfection. Marvellous. In the middle of it, the doorman called up on the housephone and asked if anybody was dancing up there. A Mr. Seligman, on the fourth—

There Zooey quit reading. He gave the stack of cardboards a solid-sounding double tap on the desk surface, as one taps a deck of cards, then dropped the stack back into the bottom drawer and closed the drawer.

Once again he leaned forward on his elbows and buried his face in his hands. This time he sat motionless for almost a half hour.

When he moved again, it was as though marionette strings had been attached to him and given an overzealous yank. He appeared to be given just enough time to pick up his cigar before another jerk of the invisible strings swung him over to the chair at the second desk in the room—Buddy's desk—where the phone was.

In this new seating arrangement, the first thing he did was to pull his shirt ends out of his trousers. He unbuttoned the shirt completely, as if the journey of three steps had taken him into an oddly tropical zone. Next, he took his cigar out of his mouth, but transferred it to his left hand and kept it there. With his right hand he took his handkerchief off his head and laid it beside the phone, in what was very implicitly a "ready position." He then picked up the phone without any perceptible hesitation and dialled a local number. A very local number indeed. When he had finished dialling, he picked up his handkerchief from the desk and put it over the mouthpiece, quite loosely and mounted rather high. He took a deepish breath, and waited. He might have lighted his cigar, which had gone out, but he didn't.

ABOUT a minute and a half earlier, Franny, on a distinctly quavering note, had just declined her mother's fourth offer within fifteen minutes to bring in a cup of "nice, hot chicken broth." Mrs. Glass had made this last offer on her feet —in fact, halfway out of the living room, in the direction of the kitchen, looking rather grim with optimism. But the reintroduced quaver in Franny's voice had sent her quickly back to her chair.

Mrs. Glass's chair was, of course, on Franny's side of the living room. And most vigilantly so. Some fifteen minutes earlier, when Franny had been rehabilitated enough to sit up and look around for her comb, Mrs. Glass had brought over the straight chair from the writing table and placed it squarely up against the coffee table. The site was excellent for Franny-observing, and also placed the observer within easy reach of an ashtray on the marble surface.

Re-seated, Mrs. Glass sighed, as she always sighed, in any situation, when cups of chicken broth were declined. But she had, so to speak, been cruising in a patrol boat down and up her children's alimentary canals for so many years that the sigh was in no sense a real signal of defeat, and she said, almost immediately, "I don't see how you expect to get your *strength* and all back if you don't take something nourishing into your system. I'm *so*rry, but I don't. You've had exactly—"

"Mother—now, please. I've asked you twenty times. Will you *please* stop mentioning chicken broth to me? It nauseates me just to—" Franny broke off, and listened. "Is that our phone?" she said.

Mrs. Glass was already up from her chair. Her lips had tightened a bit. The ring of a telephone, any telephone, anywhere, invariably caused Mrs. Glass's lips to tighten a bit. "I'll be right back," she said, and left the room. She was chinking more audibly than usual, as if a box of assorted household nails had come apart in one of her kimono pockets.

She was gone about five minutes. When she

returned, she had the particular facial expression that her eldest daughter, Boo Boo, had once
described as meaning one of only two things:
that she had just talked with one of her sons on
the telephone or that she had just had a report,
on the best authority, that the bowels of every
single human being in the world were scheduled
to move with perfect hygienic regularity for a
period of one full week. "That's Buddy on the
phone," she announced as she came into the
room. From a habit of several years' standing,
she suppressed any small token of pleasure that
might have slipped into her voice.

Franny's visible reaction to this news was considerably less than enthusiastic. She looked, in
fact, nervous. "Where's he phoning from?" she
said.

"I didn't even ask him. He sounds as though
he has a horrible cold." Mrs. Glass didn't sit
down. She hovered. "Hurry up, now, young
lady. He wants to talk to *you*."

"Did he say so?"

"*Cer*tainly he said so! Hurry up, now. . . . Put
your slippers on."

Franny let herself out of the pink sheets and
the pale-blue afghan. She sat, pale and obviously
stalling, on the couch edge, looking up at her
mother. Her feet fished around for her slippers.
"What'd you tell him?" she asked nervously.

"Just kindly go to the phone, please, young
lady," Mrs. Glass said evasively. "Just *hur*ry a
little, for goodness' sake."

"I suppose you told him I'm at death's door or something," Franny said. There was no reply to this. She stood up from the couch, not so fragilely as a post-operative convalescent might have but with just a trace of timidity and caution, as if she expected, and perhaps rather hoped, to feel a trifle dizzy. She worked her feet more securely into her slippers, then came out from behind the coffee table gravely, untying and retying the belt of her dressing gown. A year or so earlier, in an unwarrantably self-deprecating paragraph of a letter to her brother Buddy, she had referred to her own figure as "irreproachably Americanese." Watching her, Mrs. Glass, who happened to be a great judge of young girls' figures and young girls' walks, once again, in lieu of a smile, tightened her lips a bit. The instant, however, that Franny was out of sight, she turned her attention to the couch. Clearly, from her look, there were not many things in the world she disliked more than a couch, a good eiderdown couch, that had been made up for sleeping purposes. She went around into the aisle made by the coffee table and began to give all the pillows in sight a therapeutic beating up.

Franny, in transit, ignored the telephone in the hall. She evidently preferred to take the longish walk down the hall to her parents' bedroom, where the more popular phone in the apartment was located. Although there was nothing markedly peculiar about her gait as she moved through the hall—she neither dallied nor quite hurried—she was nonetheless very peculiarly transformed as she moved. She appeared, vividly, to grow younger with each step. Possibly long halls, plus the aftereffects of tears, plus the ring of a telephone, plus the smell of fresh paint, plus newspapers underfoot—possibly the sum of all these things was equal, for her, to a new doll carriage. In any case, by the time she reached her parents' bedroom door her handsome tailored tie-silk dressing gown—the emblem, perhaps, of all that is dormitorially chic and *fatale*—looked as if it had been changed into a small child's woollen bathrobe.

Mr. and Mrs. Glass's bedroom reeked, and even smarted, of freshly painted walls. The furniture had been herded into the middle of the room and covered with canvas—old, paint-flecked, organic-looking canvas. The beds, too, had been drawn in from the wall, but they had been covered with cotton bedspreads Mrs. Glass herself had provided. The phone was now on the pillow of Mr. Glass's bed. Evidently Mrs. Glass, too, had preferred it to the less private extension in the hall. The handpiece lay detached from its catch, waiting for Franny. It looked almost as dependent as a human being for some acknowledgment of its existence. To get to it, to redeem it, Franny had to shuffle across the floor through a quantity of newspapers and sidestep an empty paint bucket. When she did reach it, she didn't pick it up but merely sat down beside it on the bed, looked at it, looked away from it, and pushed back her hair. The night table that ordinarily stood alongside the bed had been moved close enough to it so that Franny could reach it without quite standing up. She put her hand under a particularly soiled-looking piece of canvas covering it and passed the hand back and forth till she found what she was looking for—a porcelain cigarette box and a box of matches in a copper holder. She lit a cigarette, then gave the phone another, long, exceedingly worried look. With the exception of her late brother Seymour, it should be noted, all her brothers had overly vibrant, not to say sinewy, voices on the telephone. At this hour, it was very possible that Franny felt deeply hesitant about taking a chance on just the timbre, let alone the verbal content, of any of her brothers' voices on the phone. However, she puffed nervously on her cigarette and, rather bravely, picked up the phone. "Hello. Buddy?" she said.

"Hello, sweetheart. How are you—are you all right?"

"I'm fine. How are you? You sound as though you have a cold." Then, when there was no immediate response: "I suppose Bessie's been *brief*ing you by the hour."

"Well—after a fashion. Yes and no. You know. Are you all right, sweetheart?"

"I'm fine. You sound funny, though. Either

you have a terrible cold or this is a terrible connection. Where are you, anyway?"

"Where am I? I'm right in my element, Flopsy. I'm in a little haunted house down the road. Never mind. Just talk to me."

Franny unplacidly crossed her legs. "I don't know exactly what you'd like to talk about," she said. "What all'd Bessie tell you, I mean?"

There was a most characteristically Buddylike pause at the other end. It was exactly the kind of pause—just a trifle rich with seniority of years—that had often tried the patience of both Franny *and* the virtuoso at the other end of the phone when they were small children. "Well, I'm not terribly sure what all she told me, sweetheart. Past a certain point, it's a little rude to go on listening to Bessie on the phone. I heard about the cheeseburger diet, you can be sure. And, of course, the Pilgrim books. Then I think I just sat with the phone at my ear, not really listening. You know."

"Oh," Franny said. She switched her cigarette over to her telephone hand and, with her free hand, reached again under the canvas cover on the night table and found a tiny ceramic ashtray, which she placed beside her on the bed. "You sound funny," she said. "Do you have a cold, or what?"

"I feel wonderful, sweetheart. I'm sitting here talking to you and I feel wonderful. It's a joy to hear your voice. I can't tell you."

Franny once again pushed back her hair with one hand. She didn't say anything.

"Flopsy? Can you think of anything Bessie may have missed? You feel like talking at all?"

With her fingers, Franny slightly altered the position of the tiny ashtray beside her on the bed. "Well," she said, "I'm a little talked out, to be *hon*est with you. Zooey's been at me all morning."

"Zooey? How is he?"

"How *is* he? He's *fine*. He's just tip*top*. I could just murder him, that's all."

"Murder him? Why? Why, sweetheart? Why could you murder our Zooey?"

"*Why?* Because I just could, that's all! He's com*plete*ly destructive. I've never met anyone so completely destructive in my life! It's just so un*nec*essary! One minute he launches this all-out attack on the Jesus Prayer—which I happen to be interested in—making you think you're some kind of neurotic *nit*wit for even being *in*terested in it. And about two minutes later he starts raving to you about how Jesus is the only person in the world he's ever had any re*spect* for —such a marvellous *mind*, and all that. He's just so er*rat*ic. I mean he goes around and around in such horrible *cir*cles."

"Tell about it. Tell about the horrible circles."

Here Franny made the mistake of giving a little exhalation of impatience—she had just inhaled cigarette smoke. She coughed. "Tell about it! It would just take me all day, that's all!" She put a hand to her throat, and waited for the wrong-passage discomfort to pass. "He's just a monster," she said. "He is! Not really a *mon*ster but—I don't know. He's so *bit*ter about things. He's bitter about re*lig*ion. He's bitter about *tele*vision. He's bitter about you and Seymour— he keeps saying you both made freaks out of us. *I* don't know. He jumps from one—"

"Why freaks? I know he thinks that. Or thinks he thinks it. But did he say why? What's his definition of a freak? He say, sweetheart?"

Just here, Franny, in apparent despair at the naïveté of the question, struck her forehead with her hand. Something she very probably hadn't done in five or six years—when, for example, halfway home on the Lexington Avenue bus, she discovered she had left her scarf back at the movies. "What's his defi*nit*ion?" she said. "He has about *forty* definitions for everything! If I sound slightly un*hinged*, that's the reason why. One minute—like last night—he says we're freaks because we were brought up to have only one set of standards. *Ten minutes later* he says *he's* a freak because he never wants to meet anybody for a drink. The only time—"

"Never wants to what?"

"Meet anybody for a *drink*. Oh, he had to go out last night and meet this television writer for a drink downtown, in the Village and all. That's what started it. He says the only people he ever really wants to meet for a drink somewhere are all either dead or unavailable. He says he never even wants to have *lunch* with anybody, even, unless he thinks there's a *good chance* it's going to turn out to be Jesus, the person—or the Buddha, or Hui-neng, or Shankaracharya, or somebody like that. You know." Franny suddenly put out her cigarette in the tiny ashtray—with some awkwardness, not having her second hand free to brace the ashtray. "You know what else he said to me?" she said. "You know what he swore up and down to me? He told me last night he once had a glass of ginger ale with Jesus in the kitchen when he was eight years old. Are you listening?"

"I'm listening, I'm listening . . . sweetheart."

"He said he was—this is exactly what he said —he said he was sitting at the table in the kitchen, all by himself, drinking a glass of ginger ale and eating sal*tines* and reading 'Dombey and Son,' and all of a sudden Jesus sat down in the other chair and asked if he could have a small glass of ginger ale. A *small* glass, mind you —that's exactly what he said. I mean he says things like that, and yet he thinks he's perfectly qualified to give *me* a lot of advice and stuff! *That's* what makes me so mad! I could just spit! I could! It's like being in a *lun*atic asylum and having another patient all dressed up as a *doc*tor come over to you and start taking your pulse or something. . . . It's just awful. He talks and talks and talks. And if he isn't *talk*ing, he's smoking his smelly cigars all over the house. I'm so sick of the smell of cigar smoke I could just roll over and *die*."

"The cigars are ballast, sweetheart. Sheer ballast. If he didn't have a cigar to hold on to, his feet would leave the ground. We'd never see our Zooey again."

There were several experienced verbal stunt pilots in the Glass family, but this last little remark perhaps Zooey alone was coördinated well enough to bring in safely over a telephone. Or so this narrator suggests. And Franny may have felt so, too. In any case, she suddenly knew that it was Zooey at the other end of the phone. She got up, slowly, from the edge of the bed. "All right, Zooey," she said. "All right."

Not quite immediately: "Beg pardon?"

"I said, all right, Zooey."

"*Zooey*? What is this? . . . Franny? You there?"

"I'm here. Just stop it now, please. I know it's you."

"What in the world are you talking about, sweetheart? What is this? Who's this Zooey?"

"*Zooey Glass*," Franny said. "Just stop it now, please. You're not being funny. As it happens, I'm just barely getting back to feeling halfway—"

"*Grass*, did you say? Zooey *Grass*? Norwegian chap? Sort of a heavyset, blond, ath—"

"All *right*, Zooey. Just stop, please. Enough's enough. You're not funny. . . . In case you're interested, I'm feeling absolutely lousy. So if there's anything special you have to say to me, please hurry up and say it and leave me *alone*." This last, emphasized word was oddly veered away from, as if the stress on it hadn't been fully intended.

There was a peculiar silence at the other end of the phone. And a peculiar reaction to it from Franny. She was disturbed by it. She sat down again on the edge of her father's bed. "I'm not going to hang *up* on you or anything," she said. "But I'm—I don't know—I'm *tired,* Zooey. I'm just exhausted, frankly." She listened. But there was no response. She crossed her legs. "You can go on like this all day, but I can't," she said. "All I am is on the receiving end. It isn't terribly pleasant, you know. You think everybody's made of iron or something." She listened. She started to speak up again but stopped when she heard the sound of a voice being cleared.

"I don't think everybody's made of iron, buddy."

This abjectly simple sentence seemed to disturb Franny rather more than a continued silence would have. She quickly reached over and picked a cigarette out of the porcelain box, but didn't prepare to light it. "Well, you'd think you did," she said. She listened. She waited. "I mean, did you call for any special reason?" she said abruptly. "I mean, did you have any special *rea*son for calling me?"

"No special reason, buddy, no special reason."

Franny waited. Then the other end spoke up again.

"I suppose I more or less called to tell you to go on with your Jesus Prayer if you want to. I mean that's your business. That's your business. It's a goddam nice prayer, and don't let anybody tell you anything different."

"I know," Franny said. Very nervously, she reached for the box of matches.

"I don't think I ever really meant to try to *stop* you from saying it. At least, I don't think I did. I don't know. I don't know *what* the hell was going on in my mind. There's one thing I *do* know for sure, though. I have no goddam authority to be speaking up like a *seer* the way I have been. We've had enough goddam seers in this family. That part bothers me. That part scares me a little bit."

Franny took advantage of the slight pause that followed to straighten her back a trifle, as though, for some reason, good posture, or better posture, might come in handy at any moment.

"It *scares* me a little bit, but it doesn't petrify me. Let's get that straight. It doesn't *pet*rify me. Because you forget one thing, buddy. When you first felt the urge, the *call,* to say the prayer, you didn't immediately start searching the four corners of the world for a master. *You came home.* You not only came *home* but you went into a goddam collapse. So if you look at it in a certain way, by rights you're only entitled to the low-grade spiritual counsel we're able to give you around here, and no more. At least you know there won't be any goddam ulterior motives in

-this madhouse. Whatever we are, we're not *fishy*, buddy."

Franny suddenly tried with one hand alone to get a light for her cigarette. She opened the matchbox compartment successfully, but one inept scratch of a match sent the box to the floor. She bent quickly and picked up the box, and let the spilled matches lie.

"I'll tell you one thing, Franny. One thing I *know*. And don't get upset. It isn't anything bad. But if it's the religious life you want, you ought to know right now that you're missing out on every single goddam religious action that's going on around this house. You don't even have sense enough to *drink* when somebody brings you a cup of consecrated chicken soup—which is the only kind of chicken soup Bessie ever brings to anybody around this madhouse. So just *tell* me, just tell me, buddy. Even if you went out and searched the whole world for a master —some guru, some holy man—to tell you how to say your Jesus Prayer properly, what good would it do you? How in *hell* are you going to recognize a legitimate holy man when you see one if you don't even know a cup of consecrated chicken soup when it's right in front of your nose? Can you tell me that?"

Franny was now sitting up rather abnormally straight.

"I'm just asking you. I'm not trying to upset you. Am I upsetting you?"

Franny answered, but her answer evidently didn't carry.

"What? I can't hear you."

"I said no. Where are you calling from? Where are you now?"

"Oh, what the hell's the difference where I am? Pierre, South Dakota, for God's sake. Listen to me, Franny—I'm sorry, don't get riled. But listen to me. I have just one or two very small things more, and then I'll quit, I promise you that. But did you know, just by the way, that Buddy and I drove up to see you in stock last summer? Did you know we saw you in 'Playboy of the Western World' one night? One god-awful *hot* night, I can tell you that. But did you know we were there?"

An answer seemed to be called for. Franny stood up, then immediately sat down. She placed the ashtray slightly away from her, as if it were very much in her way. "No, I didn't," she said. "Nobody said one single—*No,* I didn't."

"Well, we were. We were. And I'll tell you, buddy. You were good. And when I say good, I mean *good.* You held that goddam mess *up.* Even all those sunburned lobsters in the audience knew it. And now I hear you're finished with the theatre forever—I hear things, I hear things. And I remember the spiel you came back with when the season was over. Oh, you irritate me, Franny! I'm sorry, you *do.* You've made the great *start*ling goddam discovery that the acting profession's loaded with mercenaries and butchers. As I remember, you even looked like somebody who'd just been *shatt*ered because all the ushers hadn't been geniuses. What's the *matt*er with you, buddy? Where are your brains? If you've had a freakish education, at least *use* it, *use* it. You can say the Jesus Prayer from now till doomsday, but if you don't realize that the only thing that counts in the religious life is de-*tach*ment, I don't see how you'll ever even move an *inch*. Detachment, buddy, and only detachment. Desirelessness. 'Cessation from all hanker-ings.' It's this business of de*sir*ing, if you want to know the goddam truth, that makes an actor in the first place. Why're you making me tell you things you already know? Somewhere along the line—in one damn incarnation or another, if you like—you not only had a hankering to be an actor or an actress but to be a *good* one. You're stuck with it now. You can't just *walk out* on the results of your own hankerings. Cause and effect, buddy, cause and effect. The only thing you can do now, the only re*lig*ious thing you can do, is *act*. Act for God, if you want to— be *God's* actress, if you want to. What could be prettier? You can at least try to, if you want to —there's nothing wrong in *try*ing." There was a slight pause. "You'd better get busy, though, buddy. The goddam *sands* run out on you every time you turn around. I know what I'm talking about. You're lucky if you get time to sneeze in this goddam phenomenal world." There was an-other, slighter pause. "I used to worry about that. I don't worry about it very much any more. At least I'm still in love with Yorick's skull. At least I always have time enough to stay in love with Yorick's skull. I want an honorable goddam skull when I'm dead, buddy. I *hanker* after an honorable goddam skull like Yorick's. And so do *you*, Franny Glass. So do you, so do you. . . . Ah, God, what's the use of talking? You had the exact same goddam freakish upbringing I did, and if you don't know by this time what kind of *skull* you want when you're dead, and what you have to do to *earn* it—I mean if you don't *at least* know by this time that if you're an actress you're supposed to *act*, then what's the use of talking?"

Franny was now sitting with the flat of her free hand pressed against the side of her face, like someone with an excruciating toothache.

"One other thing. And that's all. I promise you. But the thing is, you raved and you bitched when you came home about the stupidity of audiences. The goddam 'unskilled laughter' coming from the fifth row. And that's right, that's right—God knows it's depressing. I'm not saying it isn't. But that's none of your business, really. That's none of your business, Franny. An artist's only concern is to shoot for some kind of perfection, and *on his own terms*, not anyone else's. You have no right to think about those things, I swear to you. Not in any real sense, anyway. You know what I mean?"

There was a silence. Both saw it through without any seeming impatience or awkwardness. Franny still appeared to have some considerable pain on one side of her face, and continued to keep her hand on it, but her expression was markedly uncomplaining.

The voice at the other end came through again. "I remember about the fifth time I ever went on 'Wise Child.' I subbed for Walt a few times when he was in a cast—remember when he was in that cast? Anyway, I started bitching one night before the broadcast. Seymour'd told me to shine my shoes just as I was going out the door with Waker. I was furious. The studio audience were all morons, the announcer was a moron, the sponsors were morons, and I just damn well wasn't going to shine my shoes for them, I told Seymour. I said they couldn't see them *any*way, where we sat. He said to shine them anyway. He said to shine them for the Fat Lady. I didn't know what the hell he was talking about, but he had a very Seymour look on his face, and so I did it. He never did tell me who the Fat Lady was, but I shined my shoes for the Fat Lady every time I ever went on the air again—all the years you and I were on the program together, if you remember. I don't think I missed more than just a couple of times. This terribly clear, clear picture of the Fat Lady formed in my mind. I had her sitting on this porch all day, swatting flies, with her radio going full-blast from morning till night. I figured the heat was terrible, and she probably had can-

cer, and—I don't know. Anyway, it seemed goddam clear why Seymour wanted me to shine my
shoes when I went on the air. It made *sense*."

Franny was standing. She had taken her hand
away from her face to hold the phone with two
hands. "He told me, too," she said into the
phone. "He told me to be funny for the Fat
Lady, once." She released one hand from the
phone and placed it, very briefly, on the crown
of her head, then went back to holding the
phone with both hands. "I didn't ever picture
her on a porch, but with very—you know—very
thick legs, very veiny. I had her in an *aw*ful
wicker chair. She had cancer, *too,* though, and
she had the radio going full-blast all day! Mine
did, too!"

"Yes. Yes. Yes. All right. Let me tell you something now, buddy. . . . Are you listening?"

Franny, looking extremely tense, nodded.

"I don't care where an actor acts. It can be in
summer stock, it can be over a radio, it can be
over *tele*vision, it can be in a goddam Broadway
theatre, complete with the most fashionable,
most well-fed, most sunburned-looking audience
you can imagine. But I'll tell you a terrible secret—Are you listening to me? *There isn't anyone out there who isn't Seymour's Fat Lady.*
That includes your Professor Tupper, buddy.
And all his goddam cousins by the dozens. There
isn't anyone *any*where that isn't Seymour's Fat
Lady. Don't you know that? Don't you know
that goddam secret yet? And don't you know—

listen to me, now—*don't you know who that Fat Lady really is?* . . . Ah, buddy. Ah, buddy. It's Christ Himself. Christ Himself, buddy."

For joy, apparently, it was all Franny could do to hold the phone, even with both hands.

For a fullish half minute or so, there were no other words, no further speech. Then: "I can't talk any more, buddy." The sound of a phone being replaced in its catch followed.

Franny took in her breath slightly but continued to hold the phone to her ear. A dial tone, of course, followed the formal break in the connection. She appeared to find it extraordinarily beautiful to listen to, rather as if it were the best possible substitute for the primordial silence itself. But she seemed to know, too, when to stop listening to it, as if all of what little or much wisdom there is in the world were suddenly hers. When she had replaced the phone, she seemed to know just what to do next, too. She cleared away the smoking things, then drew back the cotton bedspread from the bed she had been sitting on, took off her slippers, and got into the bed. For some minutes, before she fell into a deep, dreamless sleep, she just lay quiet, smiling at the ceiling.